# More
# Wishing-Chair
# Stories

Enjoy these other books by

*Enid Blyton*

The Adventures of the Wishing Chair
The Wishing-Chair Again

The Enchanted Wood
The Magic Faraway Tree
The Folk of the Faraway Tree
Adventure of the Goblin Dog

Magical Fairy Tales
Stories of Magic and Mischief
Stories of Wizards and Witches
Tales of Tricks and Treats

# Enid Blyton

# More Wishing-Chair Stories

HODDER

HODDER CHILDREN'S BOOKS
These stories first published in Great Britain in 1937, 1938 and 1952 in *Adventures of the Wishing-Chair, Sunny Stories* and *Enid Blyton's Omnibus* by George Newnes
This edition first published in 2018 by Egmont UK Limited
This edition published in 2020 by Hodder & Stoughton Limited

1 3 5 7 9 10 8 6 4 2

A CIP catalogue record for this book is available from the British Library.

ISBN 978 1 444 95950 5

Printed and bound in Great Britain by Clays Ltd, Elcograf S.p.A

The paper and board used in this book are made from wood from responsible sources.

Hodder Children's Books
An imprint of
Hachette Children's Group
Part of Hodder & Stoughton
Carmelite House
50 Victoria Embankment
London EC4Y 0DZ

An Hachette UK Company
www.hachette.co.uk
www.hachettechildrens.co.uk

# CONTENTS

# CHAPTER 1

## HOME FOR HALF-TERM

A little pixie peeped anxiously into the window of a small playroom built at the bottom of a garden. A robin flew down beside him and sang a little song.

'What's the matter, Binky? What do you want? What are you looking for?'

'I'm looking for Mollie and Peter,' said Binky. 'I've got the Wishing-Chair hidden under a bush just near here, and I'm waiting for the children to come home, so that I can get into this playroom of theirs and put the chair safely in its corner.'

'But you know that the children are away at boarding

school,' said the robin, with a little trill. 'How foolish you are!'

'I'm *not*,' said Binky. 'They're coming home at half-term, just for a few days. They told me so – and I promised to bring the chair from my mother's where I've been looking after it – hoping that perhaps it would grow its wings just for their half-term. So I'm not foolish, you see!'

'Sorry,' said the robin. 'Shall I go and find out if they are up at the house? I haven't *heard* them yet – and usually they make a lot of noise when they come home. Wait here, and I'll find out.'

He flew off. He peeped into all the windows, his perky little head on one side. There was nobody to be seen at all except the cook in the kitchen. She was busy making cakes.

'Ah – the children's favourite chocolate buns!' thought the robin. 'I can hear them now, banging at the front door. What a pity their mother isn't here to welcome them!'

Mrs Williams, the cook, hurried to the front door. Two children burst in at once, each carrying a small case. It was Mollie and Peter, home for the half-term!

'Hallo, Mrs Williams! Where's Mother?' cried Peter.

'Welcome home, Peter,' said Mrs Williams, 'and you too, Mollie. Your mother says she's very, very sorry, but she's had to go off to your granny, who's been taken ill. But she'll be home before you have to go back to school on Tuesday – and I'm to look after you.'

'Oh,' said the children, disappointed. Home didn't somehow seem like home without Mother there. They felt rather miserable.

'What about Daddy?' asked Mollie.

'He's away,' said Mrs Williams. 'Didn't your mother tell you that in her last letter?'

'Oh, yes,' said Mollie, remembering. 'I forgot. Oh dear – half-term without either Mother or Daddy – how horrid!'

'I've made you your favourite chocolate buns,' said Mrs Williams, following them indoors. 'And I've got ice-cream for you, too, and honey in the comb. And your mother says she has ordered twenty-four bottles of ginger beer and orangeade for you this weekend, and you can take it down to your playroom.'

'Oh, well – that sounds good,' said Peter, cheering up. 'We'll just pop upstairs with our things, Mrs Williams – and then what about your honey in the comb and chocolate buns? We're starving! We simply *never* get enough to eat at school, you know!'

'Rubbish!' said Mrs Williams. 'You're both as plump as can be!'

The two children went up the stairs two at a time. They stood at the landing window, looking down to the bottom of the garden. They could quite well see the roof of their playroom there. They looked at each other in excitement.

'I hope Binky is there,' said Mollie. 'Because if he is, and has got the Wishing-Chair with him, we shall be able to fly off on an adventure or two without bothering about anyone! It's always difficult to slip off in it when Mother and Daddy are at home – and we just *have* to keep the chair a secret. It would be too dreadful if it was put into a museum, and taken right away from us. It must be very, very valuable.'

'Yes. We're really very lucky to have a Wishing-Chair of our own,' said Peter. 'It's a long time since we got it now. Come on – let's put our things in our bedrooms, and then ask Mrs Williams to let us take our tea down to the playroom. Perhaps Binky is there.'

'He may be waiting outside,' said Mollie. 'He can't get in because the door is locked. I shall love to see his dear little pixie face again. We're lucky to have a pixie for a friend!'

Mrs Williams was quite pleased to let them have a tray of goodies to take down to the playroom with them. She piled it with buns and new bread and butter, and a slab of honey in the comb, biscuits, and ice-cream out of the freezer. It did look good!

'I'll take some ginger beer down under my arm,' said Peter. 'I can manage the tray too, if you'll bring the biscuits and ice-cream – they look as if they might slip about!'

'I'll get the key of the playroom too,' said Mollie, and she took it off its hook. Then, feeling excited, the two of them went carefully down the garden path, carrying everything between them. Would Binky be waiting for them?

He was, of course, because the robin had flown down to tell him that the children were coming. He hid behind some tall hollyhocks, and leapt out on them as they came up to the door of the playroom.

'Mollie! Peter! I'm here!'

'Binky! We *are* glad to see you!' said Mollie.

'Wait till I put down all this stuff and I'll give you a hug! There!'

She gave the little pixie such a hug that he almost choked. He beamed all over his face. 'Where's the key?'

he said. 'I'll open the door. I want to get the Wishing-Chair inside before anyone sees it. There's a tiresome little brownie who keeps on wanting to sit in it.'

He unlocked the door of the playroom and they all went in. Binky helped them with the food, and then ran to get the Wishing-Chair. He staggered in with it, beaming.

'I tipped that tiresome brownie off the seat, and he fell into some nettles,' said Binky. 'He shouted like anything. Well, does the chair look just the same as ever?'

'Oh, *yes*!' said Mollie, in delight, looking at the polished wooden chair. 'Your mother does keep it well polished, Binky. Did it grow its wings and fly off at all, while we were away at school this term?'

'It grew its wings once,' said Binky, 'but as I was in bed with a cold I couldn't fly off anywhere exciting in it – so I tied it to one of the legs of my bed, in case it tried to do anything silly, like flying out of the window.'

Mollie giggled. 'And did it try?' she asked.

'Oh, yes – it woke me up in the middle of the night, flapping its wings and tugging at my bed,' said Binky with a grin. 'But it couldn't get away, and in the morning its wings had gone again. So that was all right.'

'I do so hope it will grow its wings this weekend,' said Peter. 'We've only got a few days' holiday, then we go back to school again – and as Mother and Daddy are both away we really could go off on an adventure or two without any difficulty.'

'I expect it will,' said Binky, looking at the chair. He felt its legs to see if there were any bumps coming, which meant that its wings were sprouting. But he couldn't feel

any. What a pity!

Soon they were all sitting down enjoying Mrs Williams'
buns and ice-cream. It was a hot day, so they drank rather
a lot of the ginger beer.

'It won't last long if we drink it at this rate!' said Peter.
'I say – I wonder if Mrs Williams would mind if we lived
down here in the playroom all this weekend – slept here
too?'

'That *would* be fun!' said Mollie. 'I don't see why we
shouldn't. You could come too, Binky.'

It was very easy to arrange. Mrs Williams smiled and
nodded. 'Yes, you do that,' she said. 'Your mother said
I was to let you do what you liked, so long as it wasn't
anything silly. I'll take down bedding for you.'

'Oh, no,' said Peter, hurriedly. 'We'll take it all down,
Mrs Williams.' He didn't want any questions about the
Wishing-Chair! 'And, Mrs Williams, we could have all our

meals down there, if you like. We don't want anything hot, you know, in this weather. If you could give us some tins and a bottle of milk we could pick our own fruit and salad out of the garden. We shouldn't be any bother to you at all then.'

'You're no bother!' said Mrs Williams. 'But you do just what you like this weekend, so long as you're good and happy. I'll give you tins and milk and anything else you want – and don't be afraid I'll come bothering you, because I won't! I know how children like to have their own little secrets, and I shan't come snooping round!'

Well, that was grand! Now they could go and live in the playroom, and sleep there too – and if the Wishing-Chair grew its wings at any time, they would know at once! They would hear it beginning to creak, and see the bumps growing on its legs and the wings sprouting. Not a minute would be wasted!

It was fun taking down everything to the bright little playroom. Binky kept out of sight, of course, because nobody knew anything about him. He was as much of a secret as the Wishing-Chair!

'There now,' said Mollie, at last. 'Everything is ready for us – food – drink too – bedding – and a cushion and rug for you, Binky. We're going to have a lovely time! Wishing-Chair, grow your wings as soon as you can, and everything will be perfect!'

The Wishing-Chair gave the tiniest little cree-ee-eak.

'Did you hear that?' said Binky. 'Perhaps it *will* grow its wings soon. We'll have to keep a watch. Where shall we go to, if it does grow its wings?'

'Is there a Land of Lost Things, or something like that?' said Peter. 'I got into awful trouble this term because I lost my watch. Or what about going to a Land of Circuses or Fairs? I'd love to see a whole lot of those at once.'

'I never heard of those lands,' said Binky. 'Why don't we just let the chair take us somewhere on its own? It would be fun not to know where we are going!'

'*Oooh*, yes,' said Peter. 'That would be really exciting. Chair, do you hear us? Grow your wings and you can take us anywhere you like. But do, do *hurry up!*'

## CHAPTER 2
### CREE-EE-EAK

Mollie and Peter spent a very jolly evening with Binky, down in the playroom. They played snap and happy families and ludo, and all the time they watched the Wishing-Chair to see if it would grow its wings. They did *so* long to fly off on an adventure again.

But the chair stood there quietly, and when it was half-past eight the children were so sleepy that they felt they really must go to bed.

'We'd better go and have a bath up at the house,' said Peter. 'I feel dirty, travelling all the way home by train. We'll dress properly again, just in case the Wishing-Chair grows its wings and flies off with us. We'll say goodnight to Mrs Williams too, so that she doesn't feel she's got to come down to see if we're all right.'

Just as they went out of the door they saw somebody disappearing round the corner. 'Who was that peeping?' said Mollie at once. 'Quick, run and see, Peter.'

Peter raced round the corner of the playroom and saw a little brownie dive into a bush. He yelled at him.

'Hey, what do you think you are doing, peeping about

here? You wait till I catch you!'

A cheeky face looked out of the bush. 'I just want to see your chair grow wings, that's all. It's a Wishing-Chair, isn't it? Can't I watch it grow wings?'

'No, you can't,' said Peter. 'No peeping and prying in *our* garden, please! Keep out!'

The brownie made a rude face and pulled his head back into the leaves. Binky ran out of the playroom to see what the shouting was about.

'It's that brownie you told us about, the one who sat in the Wishing-Chair,' said Peter. 'Keep an eye open for him, Binky. We don't want him telling everyone our secret.'

'I'll watch,' said Binky. He yelled at the bush where the brownie had gone.

'Hey, you little snooper! If I see you again I'll tie you to a witch's broomstick and send you off to the moon!'

There was no answer. The children went off to the house to have their bath and Binky went back to the playroom.

Mrs Williams gave Peter and Mollie a jam sponge sandwich she had made, and another bottle of milk. 'Could you give us some eggs too?' asked Peter. 'Then we could boil them ourselves for breakfast on our own little stove. We wouldn't need to come in for breakfast then.'

Mrs Williams laughed. 'You're not going to bother me much, are you?' she said. 'Well, here you are, four new-laid eggs – and you'd better take a new loaf down with you, and some more butter. You're sure you'll be all right?'

'Oh, *yes*,' said Mollie. 'We love being on our own like this with Bi–'

Peter gave her such a nudge that she almost fell over.

She stopped and went red. Goodness gracious, she had almost said Binky's name! Mrs Williams didn't seem to have noticed anything, though. She added a pot of marmalade to the tray, and Peter took it.

'Well, I suppose I'll see you when you want more food!' she said. 'And not before. Have a nice time – and don't get into mischief!'

Peter and Mollie went down the garden path with the tray. Good! Now they wouldn't need to go up to the house for breakfast, so if the chair grew its wings that night they would have time for a nice long adventure!

Just as they got near the playroom they heard a noise of shouting and yelling.

'I told you I'd scold you if I found you peeping again!' they heard Binky say. 'Coming right into the playroom like that! Howl all you like, you'll get a worse scolding if you come back again. What's up with you that you won't do as you're told?'

'You horrid thing!' wept the little brownie. 'You're so very mean. You hurt me. I'll pay you out, yes, I will!'

Scold! Yell! Howl! Then came the sound of running feet and the little brownie almost bumped into the two children. He knocked the tray and an egg leapt right off it and landed on his head. It broke, and in an instant he had a cap of yellow yolk!

Mollie and Peter laughed. The little brownie couldn't think what had happened to him. 'I'll pay you out,' he cried. 'I will, I will!'

He disappeared into the tall hollyhocks, grumbling and wailing. Dear, dear – what a silly little fellow he was, to be sure!

'Well, he's gone,' said Peter. 'And so is one of our eggs. Never mind, we've still got three left, one for each of us. Hey, Binky, you've been having more trouble with that brownie, I see.'

'Yes. But I don't think he'll be back again in a hurry,' said Binky. 'I scolded him hard. I know who he is now. He's little Nose-About, a spoilt little brownie who sticks his nose into everything. I say – what a lovely sponge sandwich! Are we going to have some now?'

They sat down to have their supper. It was a lovely summer's evening, still quite light. As they sat by the doorway, munching big slices of jam sponge, a purple cloud blew up. Big drops of rain fell, and yet the sun still shone brightly, for it was not covered by the cloud.

'There's a rainbow, look!' said Mollie, and they all gazed at the lovely, shimmering rainbow that suddenly shone out in the sky. 'I do wish the chair would grow its wings, because I'd love to go to the rainbow and see if I could find a crock of gold where it touches the ground.'

'Yes, I'd like that too,' said Binky. 'I don't believe anyone has ever found the crock of gold yet. They say you have to slide right down the rainbow itself and land with a bump on the patch of ground where the crock is hidden.'

'Let's go right into the garden and see if we can spot where the rainbow-end touches,' said Mollie. So out they went, but as the end of the rainbow disappeared behind some high trees they couldn't make up their minds where it touched.

'It's miles away, anyhow,' said Peter. 'Isn't it a lovely thing? It's like a bridge of many colours.'

They heard a sudden little scuffling sound and turned quickly. 'Was that that tiresome brownie again?' said Binky, frowning. 'Anybody see him?'

Nobody had. Nobody had spied him scuttling into the playroom. Nobody saw where he went. Peter felt uneasy. 'I believe he's slipped into the playroom,' he said. 'We'd better look.'

They went in and hunted round. They looked into every corner, and Mollie even looked inside the doll's house because she thought he *might* have been able to squeeze himself in at the door.

'He's not in the playroom,' said Peter at last. 'We've looked simply everywhere. Let's shut the door now, and keep him out. It's still very light, and the rainbow is still lovely, though not so bright as it was. We'd better go to bed. I'm really sleepy.'

Mollie looked longingly at the Wishing-Chair. 'If only it would grow its wings!' she said. 'I just *feel* like an adventure!'

The two children had mattresses to lie on. Binky had a

cushion and a rug. They all settled down, yawning. How lovely the very first evening was! Half-term seemed to be quite long when it was still only the first day.

Mollie fell asleep first. Binky gave an enormous yawn, and then he fell asleep too. Peter lay watching the rainbow fading gradually. He could see part of it through the window.

His eyes fell shut. His thoughts went crooked, and he was *almost* asleep when something woke him.

'Creeeee-eak!'

Peter opened his eyes. What was that noise that had slipped into his first moment of dreaming? His eyes shut again.

'Cree-ee-ee-EAK!'

Ah! That woke up Peter properly. He sat up quickly. He knew that noise all right! It was made by the Wishing-Chair. It was about to grow its lovely red wings. He sat and stared at the chair.

Could he see bumps coming on its legs? He was almost sure he could. Yes – there was a big one on the right front leg – and now another on the left. He could see bumps on the back legs too.

Then one bump sprouted a few green feathers! Hurrah! The Wishing-Chair *was* growing its wings for them. What luck!

Peter reached over to Binky and gave him a little shake. He did the same to Mollie. 'Wake up! The chair's growing its wings. We can fly off on it tonight!'

Both Mollie and Binky woke up with a jump. Binky leapt up and ran to the chair. His face beamed at them.

'Yes! Look at its lovely wings sprouting out – good big

ones! Quick, open the door, and we'll all get into the chair – and away we'll go!'

Peter flung the door open. Binky and Mollie were already sitting in the chair. It flapped its wings and rose a few inches. 'Wait for Peter!' cried Mollie, in a fright. Peter leapt across to the chair and sat himself firmly on the seat. Binky sat himself on the back to make more room. Ah – they were off!

'Tell the chair where to go,' said Peter. 'Or shall we just let it take us where it wants to?'

'Chair, go to the rainbow!' suddenly cried a voice, and the chair, which was flying in the opposite direction, changed its course and flew towards the almost-faded rainbow. It had flown right out of the door and up into the air, the children and Binky holding fast to it, all feeling very excited.

'Who said that?' asked Peter. 'Did you, Mollie? Or you, Binky?'

They both said no. All three gazed at one another, puzzled. Then who *had* said it? There was nobody on the chair but themselves. Whose voice had commanded the chair to go to the rainbow?

'I expect it was that silly little brownie, calling from the ground,' said Peter at last. 'He must have seen us flying off, and yelled out to the chair to go to the rainbow. Well – shall we go?'

'Might as well,' said Binky. 'Go on, Chair – go to the rainbow!'

And immediately a voice chimed in: 'That's what *I* said! Go to the rainbow, Chair!'

Who could it be? And where was the speaker? How very, very peculiar!

## CHAPTER 3
## AN ADVENTUROUS NIGHT

'There must be somebody invisible on the chair with us!' said Binky. 'Quick – feel about on the seat and on the arms and back. Feel everywhere – and catch hold of whoever it is.'

Well, they all felt here and there, but not one of them could feel anybody. They heard a little giggle, but it was quite impossible to find whoever it was giggling.

'Surely the chair itself can't have grown a voice – and a giggle,' said Peter at last.

'Of course not. It wouldn't be so silly,' said Binky. 'Gracious – here we are at the rainbow already!'

So they were. They landed right on the top of the shimmering bow. 'It's like a coloured, curving bridge,' said Mollie, putting her foot down to it. 'Oh, Peter – we can walk on it. I never, never thought of that.'

She jumped down to the rainbow – and immediately she gave a scream.

'Oh, it's slippery! I'm sliding down! Oh, Peter, help me!'

Sure enough, poor Mollie had sat down with a bump, and was slithering down the curving rainbow at top speed.

'Follow her, Chair, follow her!' yelled Peter.

'No, don't!' shouted the strange voice, and the chair stopped at once. That made Peter angry. He began to yell at the top of his voice.

'You do as *I* tell you, Chair. Follow Mollie, follow Mollie, follow Mollie, follow …'

And because his voice was loud and he shouted without stopping, the chair couldn't hear the other little voice that called to it to stop. It slid down the rainbow headlong after Mollie, who was now nearly at the bottom. Binky held on tightly, looking scared. Would the chair be able to stop at the bottom of the rainbow?

It wouldn't have been able to stop, that was certain – but before it reached the bottom it spread its red wings and flew right off the rainbow, hovering in the air before it flew down to Mollie.

'That was clever of it,'

said Peter, with a sigh of relief. 'Mollie, are you all right?'

'I fell on a tuffet of grass, or I'd have had a dreadful bump,' said Mollie. 'Let me get on to the chair again. I don't want it to fly off without me. Oh – what's this?'

She pointed to something half-buried in the grass. It had a handle at one side, and she gave it a tug. Something bright and shining flew out of it.

'Mollie! It's the crock of gold!' shouted Peter. The one that is hidden where the rainbow-end touches. We've found it! All because you slid all the way down and landed by it with a bump. Let's pull it up.'

He and Binky jumped off the chair to go to Mollie. All three took hold of the handle of the crock and tugged. It came up out of the ground with a rush, and all three fell over.

'There it is – and, my word, it's *full* of gold!' said Peter. He put his hand into the crock and ran the gold through his fingers. 'Who would have thought we would be the first to find the gold at the rainbow's end?'

'Let's carry it to the chair and take it with us,' said Mollie. 'I don't know what we're going to do with it, though! We could give it away bit by bit to all the poor people we meet, perhaps.'

They lifted the gold on to the seat of the nearby Wishing-Chair. They were just about to climb on beside it when the strange little voice cried out again.

'Off you go, Wishing-Chair! Go to the Brownie Mountain!'

The chair rose up, flapping its wings. It almost got away – but Peter managed to catch hold of the bottom of its right front leg. He held on for all he was worth, and Mollie helped him. They pulled the chair down between them, and climbed on to it.

'This is amazing!' said Binky. 'Who is it that keeps calling out? Where *can he* be? Even if he is invisible we should be able to *feel* him! He nearly got away with the chair, and the gold too. My word, if I get hold of him I'll turn him into a fly and blow him into a spider's web!'

'Chair, go to the Old Woman Who Lives in a Shoe!' cried the voice suddenly, and the chair shot off to the east.

'Oh, no!' yelled Peter, angrily. 'We're not going there for the Old Woman to get hold of us. Chair, go where you like!'

The chair set off to the west, then, changing its course so suddenly that Binky almost fell off the back, it flew over a land of gleaming towers.

Binky peered down. 'This is the Land of Bells, I think,' he said. 'There are bells in every tower. Yes, listen – you can hear them.'

'Ding-dong, dong-dong, dell!' rang dozens and dozens of bells, echoing all through the sky round them. The Wishing-Chair didn't attempt to go down. It kept high above the tall, gleaming towers, and soon it had left the Land of Bells far behind.

'It's beginning to get really dark now,' said Peter, peering down. 'Where do you suppose the chair is going to?'

'I think it's rather cross,' said Binky. 'It's begun to creak a bit. I wonder why? We haven't done anything to make it angry. I wish it wouldn't swing about so. It feels as if it's trying to shake us off.'

'Yes, it does,' said Mollie. 'Hold tight, everyone! I say, look – is that a town down there? Binky, do you know what it is?'

Binky peered down. 'Yes – it's the Town of Bad Dreams. Goodness, I hope we don't go there. We don't want to fall into a bad dream and not know how to get out of it!'

'Go on farther, Chair,' commanded Peter at once. A little voice called out too, 'Go farther! Go to the Brownie Mountain!'

'There's that voice again,' said Binky crossly. 'Chair, take no notice. You belong to *us* and you have to do what *we* say! Go farther – but go where you like. We want an adventure before we go back home.'

The chair suddenly began to drop downwards. Binky peered to see where they were going. 'We've passed the Town of Bad Dreams. We're dropping down to the Village of Gobbo. Yes – that's right. Dear me, I wonder why? Gobbo is the head of all the brownies, and bad ones are sent to him to be punished.'

A loud wail rose in the air. 'Oh my, oh my! Chair, go to the Brownie Mountain, I tell you!'

But the chair took no notice. It flew right down to the ground, and immediately two stern-looking brownies came up, both with long beards and shaggy eyebrows.

'Who has been brought to be punished?' said one. 'Which one of you is a bad brownie?'

'Not one of us,' said Peter, puzzled. 'Mollie and I are children – and Binky here is a pixie.'

'Well, go away again, then,' said one of the brownies. 'Landing is not allowed here unless naughty brownies are to be taken before our chief, Gobbo.'

'Right. Chair, fly away again,' said Peter. Up flew the chair – but one of the brownies suddenly gave a loud cry and caught hold of the right-hand wing. The chair almost tipped over, and Binky fell right off the back. He landed with a bump on the ground.

'What did you do that for?' he shouted to the brownie. Then he stared in surprise. The two brownies pulled the children off the chair, which was now back again on the ground – and then they turned the chair upside down! It creaked angrily.

'Don't do that!' said Peter, astonished. Then he stared, even more astonished! Underneath the chair, clinging desperately to it, was the naughty little brownie who had peeped and pried outside the playroom!

'Look at that!' cried Mollie. 'It's Nose-About, the

tiresome brownie! He must have slipped into the playroom and clung to the underneath of the chair so that we couldn't see him. And he flew off with us, and tried to make the chair go where *he* wanted to.'

'And when we found the rainbow gold he wanted to go off to Brownie Mountain with it. That's where he lives, I expect,' said Peter. 'It was his voice we kept hearing! He was underneath the seat of the chair all the time.'

'No wonder the chair took us to the Village of Gobbo, then,' said Binky. 'It knew he was under it and wanted him to be punished. Brownies, take him away. He's a nuisance.'

'No, no! Mercy, mercy!' wept the little brownie. 'Forgive me! I just wanted a ride, that's all. And when I saw the gold I thought I'd make the chair go to my home with it – then I'd be rich all my life.'

'You're very bad and you want punishing,' said Peter. 'I'm not at all sorry for you.'

'One punishment every day for a month,' said one of the brownies, solemnly, clutching hold of the frightened brownie. 'And he will never be allowed to go back home.'

The little brownie wailed loudly. 'But my mother will miss me so. She loves me, she does really. I do lots of jobs for her. And my little sister loves me too. I take her to school each day. Do, do let me go. I only wanted the gold for my mother.'

Mollie suddenly felt sorry for him. She knew how much *her* mother would miss her if she were taken away. And perhaps this naughty little brownie was quite good and kind at home.

She put her hand on the arm of one of the brownies. 'Let him go, please. He's sorry now. He won't be bad again.'

'Oh, yes, he will,' said the brownie. 'He's growing into a perfect nuisance. We'll soon cure him.'

'No, no, no,' wailed the little brownie. 'Let me go. I want my mother, I do, I do.'

'How much will you charge us for letting him go?' asked Mollie, much to Peter's surprise.

The two brownies talked together about this. 'Well,' said one at last, 'our master, the Great Gobbo, is laying out some wonderful rose-gardens, but he hasn't enough money to finish them. We will let this brownie go if you pay us a fine of one thousand gold pieces. And that's cheap!'

'It isn't,' said Mollie. 'Peter, help me to count out the gold in this crock. I don't think there are as many as a thousand pieces, though. We'll just see.'

They all began to count, the little brownie too. They counted one hundred – then two – then three and four and five and, will you believe it, in that rainbow-crock there were exactly one thousand and one pieces of gold!

'There you are – a thousand pieces,' said Peter, handing them over. 'We'll have the odd one – and the crock too, because it will look nice on our playroom mantelpiece. Now can we go?'

'Yes, certainly,' said the brownies, delighted. 'But we must warn this little brownie that *next* time the fine will be *two* thousand pieces! Goodbye!'

'Goodbye,' called everyone, and up went the Wishing-

Chair into the air again. Where to next?

'Thank you,' said the small brownie, in a humble voice. 'Thank you very much. Please drop me at Brownie Mountain, will you?'

## CHAPTER 4

## LAND OF WISHES

'Well, brownie, you were lucky to have a kind friend like Mollie to pay your fine,' said Binky, who wasn't really very pleased about it at all. 'Behave yourself, please – or I shall tell you mother all about you.'

The chair was a bit crowded now, with the two children, the brownie, and the pixie, and the empty crock as well. Peter had the one piece of gold that was left. He had put it into his pocket.

'I'll take you to the Land of Wishes if you like,' said the small brownie, humbly. He was very anxious to please them all now. 'You can have as many wishes as you like this weekend because it's Princess Peronel's birthday. I've an invitation ticket. Look.'

He pulled a rather crumpled ticket from his pocket. It certainly was an invitation.

'But it's for you, not for us,' said Peter.

'It says "For Brownie Nose-About *and Friends*",' said the brownie. 'I'm Nose-About – and you're my friends, aren't you? Oh, please do say you are!'

'Well – all right, we're your friends then,' said Peter.

'Mollie certainly *was* a friend to you in the Village of Gobbo! Binky, shall we go to the Land of Wishes? I know quite a few wishes I'd like to wish!'

'Yes, let's go,' said Binky. 'Nose-About, *you'd* better tell the chair to go, because you're the one who has the invitation.'

So, in a rather important voice, Nose-About told the chair where to go. 'To the Land of Wishes, please,' he said. 'To the Princess Peronel's birthday party.'

The chair gave a little creak and flew straight upwards. It was very dark now and stars were out in the sky. Mollie began to feel sleepy. She nodded her head and leant against Peter. Peter nodded his head too, and both of them slept soundly. Binky and Nose-About kept guard. The chair flew all night long, for the Land of Wishes was a long, long way away.

The sun was up and the sky was full of light when at last the two children awoke. Below them was a land of flowers and lakes and streams and shining palaces. How lovely!

'Does *everyone* live in a palace here?' asked Mollie, marvelling at so many palaces.

'Oh, yes. It's easy enough to wish for one,' said Nose-About, peering down. 'And then when you're tired of living in an enormous place with windows everywhere, you just wish for a rose-covered cottage. Would you like a palace for a bit? I'll wish you one!'

The chair flew downwards. It landed in a field of shining, star-like flowers. 'Here we are,' said the brownie. 'I'll wish for a palace to begin with – and then we can be princes and a princess, and go to Princess Peronel's birthday party.

I wish for a palace with one thousand and one windows!'

And silently and shimmeringly a tall, slender palace rose up round them. The sun shone in through hundreds of windows.

'I'll just count if there *are* a thousand and one,' said Nose-About.

'Oh, *no*! We simply *can't* count up to a thousand and one all over again!' groaned Peter. 'I say – look at the Wishing-Chair. It's standing on that platform there wishing it was a throne!'

'I wish it *was* a throne!' said Mollie at once. And dear me, the good old Wishing-Chair changed into a gleaming throne, with a big red velvet cushion on its seat and tassels hanging down its back. It looked very grand indeed.

Peter went and sat on it. 'I wish I was a prince!' he said. And to Mollie's enormous surprise her brother suddenly looked like a very handsome little prince, with a circlet of gold round his head and a beautiful cloak hanging from his velvet-clad shoulders. He grinned at Mollie. 'Better wish yourself to be a princess before I order you about!' he said. 'I feel like giving a whole lot of orders! Where's my horse? Where are my dogs? Where are my servants?'

Well, before very long Mollie was a princess, and looked quite beautiful in a dress that swept the ground and twinkled with thousands of bright jewels as she walked. Binky wished himself a new suit and a new wand. Nose-About still felt very humble so he didn't wish for anything for himself but only things for the others.

He wished for horses and dogs and cats and servants and ice-creams and everything he could think of.

'I think we've got enough dogs, Nose-About,' said Peter at last. 'And I'd rather not have any more ice-creams. I feel rather as if I'd like a good breakfast. All the clocks you wished for have just struck nine o'clock. I feel hungry.'

The brownie wished for so much porridge and bacon and eggs that there was enough for the cats and dogs too. The servants had taken the horses out of the palace, which made Mollie feel more comfortable, because when the brownie had first wished for them they kept galloping round the enormous room. She was afraid of being knocked over.

That was a most exciting morning. When the children got into the way of wishing there was no end to the things they thought of!

'I feel like snowballing! I wish for plenty of snow!' said Peter, suddenly. And outside the palace windows fell the snowflakes, thick and fast. There was soon enough for a game. It was very easy to wish the snow away when they were tired of snowballing and wish for something else – an aeroplane they could fly, or a train they could drive.

'I wish this would last all over our weekend,' sighed Mollie. 'I'm enjoying it so.'

'Well – I suppose it will,' said Peter, 'Now you've wished it, the wish will come true. But what about Mother? She won't like it if we stay away all the time.'

'I'll wish *her* here, then,' said Mollie. But Peter wouldn't let her.

'No. Don't,' he said. 'If she's with Granny she wouldn't like leaving her – and it would upset Granny to see Mother suddenly disappear. We'll just enjoy ourselves here, and then try and explain to Mother when we get home.'

The princess's party was wonderful. It began at four o'clock that afternoon, and lasted till past midnight. There was a birthday cake that was so very big it took six little servants to cut it into slices. One hundred candles burnt on it! How old Peronel must be!

'A hundred years old is *young* for a fairy,' said Binky. 'See how beautiful the princess still is.'

She certainly was. Peter wished hard for a dance with her – and at once she glided over to him, and danced as lightly as a moth. 'Now I can say I've danced with a princess!' thought Peter, pleased.

The next day came and slid away happily. Then the next day and the next. The children grew used to having every single wish granted.

'A big chocolate ice at once!' And hey presto! it came. 'A tame lion to ride on!' There it was, purring like a cat. 'Wings on my back to fly high above the trees!' And there they were, fluttering strongly, carrying Mollie high in the air. What a truly lovely feeling.

On that fourth day the children didn't wish quite so many things. 'Tired of wishing?' asked Binky, who hadn't really wished many things. 'Ah – people always get tired of wishes coming true after a time.'

'I can't seem to think of any more,' said Peter.

'I keep thinking of Mother,' said Mollie. 'I do so hope she isn't worried about us. We've got to go back home today, Peter – do you realise that? It's the day we have to go back to school. It's a pity we've had so little time at home. We shall hardly have seen Daddy and Mother at all.'

'Oh goodness – how the weekend has flown,' said Peter. 'I wanted to do quite a lot of things at home too. I wanted to get out my electric train – and didn't you want to take your dolls out just once in their pram, Mollie?'

'Yes, I did,' said Mollie. 'Oh dear – I do wish we had the weekend in front of us still, so that we could enjoy being at home too! I feel as if we've rather wasted it now. Peter, I think we ought to go back. We've a train to catch, you know. We mustn't be late back for school.'

'All right. Binky, we'd better change the throne back to the Wishing-Chair,' said Peter. 'Wish for its wings, will you? They've gone, but a wish will bring them back, in the Land of Wishes!'

It did, of course. As soon as the throne had changed back into the Wishing-Chair they knew so well, Binky wished for the wings to grow – and they sprouted out gaily, at once, looking bigger than ever.

'You coming, Nose-About?' said Peter to the little brownie.

'No. I'm going back home to my mother,' he said. 'Goodbye. Thank you for being kind to me.'

'Well, you've certainly repaid our kindness!' said Mollie. 'I've never had such a wonderful time in my life. Now – are we all ready? Wishing-Chair, home, please, as fast as you can!'

It was a long, long way back from the Land of Wishes. They all three went sound asleep, and the chair was careful not to jolt them at all in case they fell off. It flew

32

down to the playroom at last, and went in gently at the door. It tipped out Mollie and Peter on to their mattresses, and Binky on to his cushion. The crock that had contained the rainbow gold tipped out too, and fell on to the carpet. Luckily it didn't break.

The children groaned a little, and then slept on soundly, curled up on their mattresses. The chair stood still. Its red wings disappeared gradually. It was just a chair.

And then there came a loud knocking at the door, and a loud voice too.

'Peter! Mollie! How late you are sleeping! Haven't you had your breakfast yet? Your mother has telephoned to say that Granny is much better and she'll be home to lunch. Isn't that good news?'

The children woke up with a jump and stared at Mrs Williams' smiling face. She was looking in at the door. Peter sat up and rubbed his eyes. 'Well, I declare!' said Mrs Williams. 'You are not in your night-things! You don't mean to say you didn't go to bed properly last night? Do wake up. It's half-past ten already!'

'Half-past ten?' said Mollie, amazed. 'What day is it, Mrs Williams?'

'Saturday, to be sure!' said Mrs Williams, surprised. 'You came home yesterday, that was Friday – and so today's Saturday!'

'But – but surely it's Tuesday or perhaps even Wednesday,' said Mollie, remembering the wonderful weekend in the Land of Wishes. 'Aren't we due back at school?'

'Bless us all, you're asleep and dreaming!' said Mrs

Williams. 'Well, I must be getting on with my work. It's Saturday morning, half-past ten, and your mother will be home for lunch. Now – do you understand *that*?'

And off she went, quite puzzled. She hadn't seen Binky on the cushion. He was still fast asleep!

Mollie looked at Peter and her eyes shone. 'Peter, oh Peter!' she said. 'Do you remember that I wished we had the weekend in front of us still? Well, that wish has come true too. We've *had* the weekend once in our palace – and now we're going to have it all over again at home. Could anything be nicer!'

'Marvellous!' said Peter, jumping up. 'Simply marvellous! Wake up, you lazy old Binky. We've good news for you. It's not Tuesday – it's only Saturday!'

So there they are, just going to welcome their mother back again, and looking forward to a wonderful half-term.

'Crreee-eee-eak!' says the good old Wishing-Chair, happily.

## CHAPTER 5

## SANTA CLAUS AND THE WISHING-CHAIR

Christmas was coming. Peter and Mollie were home from boarding school and were very excited.

'Two more days till Christmas!' said Peter. 'Then stockings, and crackers, and pudding, and a Christmas tree, and parties. Oooh!'

The next day came – and that was Christmas Eve. 'Only today,' said Mollie, 'then Christmas!'

They went down to their playroom, which was built at the bottom of the garden. The Wishing-Chair was there, but Binky, their friend, was not. He had gone Christmas shopping.

'Binky said he would hang his stocking up on the back of the Wishing-Chair,' said Mollie. 'Then Santa Claus would fill it for him. Where shall we put the presents we have bought for him, Peter?'

They put them on the sofa in the corner, and then ran back to the house. They had not been for any rides on the Wishing-Chair so far these holidays – but they had been so busy doing their Christmas shopping that they had hardly paid any attention to the magic chair.

The children hung up their stockings that night at the end of their beds. Mother tucked them up, kissed them, and put out the light.

'Now, go to sleep quickly,' she said. 'No staying awake and peeping.'

So they went straight off to sleep, and began to dream about parties and presents. But in the middle of the night, Peter suddenly woke up. He had heard a strange noise in his sleep. What could it be?

It was someone tapping on the windowpane outside. Tap-tap-tap! Tap-tap-tap!

'Mollie! Wake up!' cried Peter. 'There's someone knocking at the window.'

Mollie sat up, rubbing her eyes.

'Do you suppose it's Santa Claus?' she said, in an excited voice.

'Of course not! He comes down the chimney,' said Peter. 'Come on. Let's see who it is.'

They went to the window and opened it – and in popped Binky the pixie, shivering with cold, and panting with excitement.

'Mollie! Peter! Something's happened! I was asleep in the playroom when I heard a galloping noise – and I looked out of the window. And I saw Santa Claus and his reindeer in the sky, and the reindeer were running away. Something had frightened them. Then I heard a crash, and I'm sure the reindeer have galloped into some trees and broken the sleigh. Will you come with me and see?'

The children dressed quickly, for it was a cold night. They

put on their warmest coats and crept downstairs. Soon they were at the bottom of the garden. The moon came out from behind a cloud and lit up everything for them.

'It's nearly midnight,' said Binky. 'I do hope Santa Claus hasn't been hurt.'

He hurried them into the field at the back of the garden and ran towards some big elm trees – and there they saw a strange sight.

The sleigh and the reindeer had got caught in the trees. The children and Binky could quite clearly see them in the moonlight.

'Oh dear,' said Mollie, half frightened. 'I wonder where Santa Claus is?'

'There's somebody climbing down the tree – look!' said Binky. So there was – and even as the children watched, someone jumped down from the tree and came towards them.

'It's Santa Claus,' said Peter. Sure enough, it was. There was no mistake about it, for there were the bright twinkling eyes, the snow-white beard, and the red, hooded coat.

'Good evening, sir,' said Binky. 'I'm afraid you've had an accident.'

'I certainly have,' said Santa Claus, in a worried voice. 'Something frightened my reindeer and they ran away at top speed. They ran into the top of that tall tree and wrecked my sleigh. Now what am I to do? It's Christmas night and I've thousands of stockings to fill.'

Santa Claus still had his sack with him, and it was bulging full of toys. He put it down on the ground and wiped his hot forehead.

'What will happen to the poor reindeer?' asked Mollie.

'Oh, I've sent a message to my reindeer stables, and they will send along two or three men to free them from the branches and take them home,' said Santa Claus. 'And now the next thing is – what will happen to *me*? Here am I, Santa Claus, with a big sack of toys to fill everyone's stockings – and no way to get to those stockings.'

It was then that Peter had his wonderful idea. He nearly cried with excitement as he spoke.

'Santa Claus, oh, Santa Claus! *I* know what you can do. Borrow our Wishing-Chair.'

'Whatever is the boy talking about?' said Santa Claus, puzzled. 'Wishing-Chair! There aren't such things nowadays.'

'Well, *we've* got one,' said Mollie, overjoyed at Peter's idea. 'Come on, Santa. We'll take you to where we keep it, and then you'll see for yourself. You could fly in it to every chimney quite easily.'

They dragged the big jolly man across the field and through the hedge into their garden. Binky was just as excited as everyone else. They all went into the playroom and Binky lit the lamp.

'There you are,' he said proudly, holding the lamp over the old Wishing-Chair. 'There's the wonderful chair. And look! It's grown its wings all ready to take you, Santa. It might have known you were coming.'

Santa stared at the rose-red wings that were slowly flapping to and fro on the legs of the chair. His eyes shone in the lamplight.

'Yes,' he said. 'Yes. The very thing. I didn't know there was a Wishing-Chair in the world nowadays. May I really borrow it, children?'

'Yes,' said Mollie.

'On one condition,' said Peter, suddenly.

'What's that?' asked Santa Claus, putting his great bag over his shoulder.

'Take us with you in the chair for just a little while so that we can see how you slip down the chimneys and into the bedrooms,' begged Peter. 'Oh do!'

'But will the chair hold all of us?' said Santa doubtfully. 'I'm rather heavy, you know.'

'Oh, the chair is as strong as ten horses,' said Binky eagerly. 'You don't know the adventures it has had, Santa. Get in, and we'll go.'

Santa sat down in the chair. He filled it right up. He took Mollie on his knee. Binky climbed to the back of the chair, where he always sat – and Peter sat on the sack of toys. The chair gave a creak, flapped its wings fast, and rose into the air.

'We're off!' cried Mollie, in excitement. 'Oh, who would have thought that we'd be flying to the housetops with Santa Claus tonight. What a fine adventure we'll have!'

The Wishing-Chair rose high into the air once it got out of doors. Mollie shivered, for the air was frosty. Santa Claus covered her up with part of his wide coat. They passed the elm tree where the sleigh and the reindeer had got caught.

'Look,' said Peter. 'There are your men freeing the reindeer from the branches, Santa Claus.'

'Good!' said Santa. 'They will be quite all right now. Hallo, the chair is flying down to this roof. Who lives here, children?'

'Frannie and Tommy Dawson,' said Peter. 'Oh, have you got presents for their stockings, Santa? They are such nice, kind children.'

'Yes, I know,' said Santa, looking at a big notebook where many names were written down. 'Ah! Frannie wants two twin dolls and a puzzle, and Tommy wants a train and some lines. Put your hand into the sack, Peter, please, and take them out.'

Peter put his hand into the enormous sack, and the first things he felt were the dolls, the puzzle, and the train with lines! He pulled them out.

'You might see if there are any oranges and nuts there too,' said Santa. 'I always like to give a little extra something to good children.'

Peter put his hand into the sack again and felt a handful of nuts, apples and oranges. He gave them to Santa. The chair flew down to a flat piece of roof just by a big chimney. Santa put Mollie off his knee and stood up.

'Watch me slip down this chimney!' he said – and in a second he was gone! It was astonishing how such a big man could get down the chimney.

'Quick!' said Binky, patting the chair. 'Get in, Mollie. We'll fly the chair down to Frannie's window and peep in to see what Santa Claus does there. He won't mind.'

The chair rose off the roof and flew down to a little window. It put two of its legs there and balanced itself most unsafely, flapping its wings all the time so that it wouldn't fall. Binky and the children peered in at the window.

Frannie and Tommy always had a night-light, and they could see the room quite clearly. Frannie was asleep in her cot, and Tommy was asleep in his small bed.

'Look! There's Santa's feet coming out of the fireplace!' said Binky excitedly. 'Don't they look funny! And now there's his knees – and his waist – and all of him. It's funny he doesn't get black!'

Santa Claus slipped right out of the fireplace and tiptoed to Frannie's bed. There was a stocking hanging at the end. Santa put the oranges, apples and nuts at the bottom, and then stuffed in the puzzle and the twin dolls.

Frannie didn't stir! She was quite sound asleep. Santa Claus went to Tommy next and filled his stocking too. Then he tiptoed back to the chimney, put his head up, and was soon lost to sight. The Wishing-Chair flew back to the roof and waited there for Santa. Up he came, puffing and blowing.

'I saw you peeping in at the window!' he said. 'You gave me quite a fright at first. Come along now – to the next house where there are children!'

It was not far off, for Harry and Ronald, two big boys, lived next door! Santa looked them up in his notebook and found that they were good, clever boys. Neither of them had asked for anything in their stockings. They had just left it to Santa Claus to choose for them.

'Now, let me see,' said Santa. '*Clever* boys, my notebook says. What about a book on aeroplanes for Harry, and a big meccano set – and a book on ships for Ronald, and a really difficult puzzle? Put your hand in the sack, Peter, and see what you can find.'

Peter slipped in his hand – and, of course, he found the books, the meccano, and the puzzle at once! It almost seemed as if the toys arranged themselves just right for Santa Claus! It was part of his magic, Peter supposed.

He handed the things out to Santa Claus, and then took apples, nuts, oranges and a few crackers from the sack too. Santa Claus got off the chair and went down the chimney again.

'Come on, Chair,' said Mollie. 'Let's go and peep in at the window again!'

So the chair flew down to the window-sill and tried to balance itself. Harry and Ronald had no night-light, but the moon shone well in at their window, and the children and Binky could easily see what was happening inside.

They saw Santa creep out of the chimney, and go to Harry's stocking – and then, just as Santa was turning to go to Ronald's bed, the Wishing-Chair fell off the window-sill. The sill was very narrow indeed, and the chair simply couldn't stay there!

The children gave a small squeal, for they were frightened when the chair fell. Of course, it at once rose up again to the roof, flapping its strong wings. But the noise had awakened Ronald, and he sat up!

The children didn't see what happened, but Santa Claus told them when he at last came up the chimney once more.

'You shouldn't have made such a noise,' he said. 'You woke Ronald, and I had to hide behind a chair till he lay down and went to sleep again!' I might have had to wait for an hour!'

'We're very sorry,' said Binky. 'The chair slipped and we thought we were falling! Perhaps we'd better not peep in at the windows any more.'

'I suppose we couldn't come down a chimney with you, could we?' asked Mollie longingly. 'I've always wanted to do that.'

'Yes, you can if you like,' said Santa, 'but you must not make any noise. Now, who's next on the list? Oh, Joy Brown, seven years old.'

Nobody said anything, but Mollie and Peter thought a lot. Joy was not a bit like her name – she was a spiteful, unkind child, who didn't bring joy to anyone. Mollie was surprised that Santa Claus should take presents to Joy.

But he wasn't going to! He read a few lines out loud and then pursed up his mouth. 'Dear, dear! Joy seems to be a bad girl. Listen to this! "Joy Brown – unkind, selfish, and never gives any happiness to anyone. Does not deserve any toys this Christmas." Well, well, well – we must miss her out, I'm afraid.'

So the Wishing-Chair flew past Joy's house. There was nothing in that naughty little girl's stocking the next morning!

'This is George's house,' said Peter eagerly, as the chair flew down on to a sloping roof. It was so sloping that they all had to hold on to the nearest chimney. 'Can't we go down with you, Santa?'

Santa nodded, so Mollie tried to get into the chimney. But she stuck fast and couldn't go down! Then Peter tried, but he stuck fast too, and so did Binky. Santa Claus laughed softly.

'Ah! You don't know my trick! I could never get down some of these narrow chimneys if I didn't use some magic oil to make the chimney slippery! In the old days chimneys were very wide and there was no difficulty, but nowadays the chimneys are narrow and small. Stand back, Binky, and I'll pour a little of my oil down.'

Santa Claus tipped a small bottle up, and a few drops fell down the chimney. 'Now try, Mollie,' said Santa.

So Mollie tried again, and this time she slid down the chimney quite easily, and crept out of the bottom into George's bedroom! It did seem strange! There was George in bed, and he was snoring very gently, so Mollie knew he must be asleep.

Then Peter slid down, then Binky, and last of all Santa Claus. 'You can fill George's stocking if you like,' he whispered to Peter. 'You're a friend of George's, aren't you? I know you like him very much.'

'Yes, he's a fine boy,' said Peter, and he took the books, the fruit, and the box of small motor cars that Santa gave him. Soon George's stocking was full to the top!

'It's fun playing at being Santa Claus!' said Peter. Then they all crept up the chimney again, but Binky had a dreadful time trying not to sneeze, because the soot got up his nose and tickled it.

'A-tishoo!' he said, when he stood on the roof again, holding firmly to a chimney. 'A-tishoo!'

'Sh!' said Santa in alarm. 'Don't do that!'

'A-tishoo!' said poor Binky. 'I can't help it. A-tishoo!'

Santa Claus bundled him into the chair and they all flew off to another house. 'Now this must be the last house you visit with me,' said Santa Claus, seeing Mollie yawning and rubbing her eyes. 'You must be fresh and lively on Christmas Day, or people will wonder what is the matter with you. You may come down the chimney here, and then I shall fly back to your own house with you, and go on my journey by myself!'

The children and Binky were disappointed, but they knew Santa was right. They really were beginning to feel very sleepy. They slipped down the chimney with Santa, and Mollie filled Angela's stocking herself with all kinds of exciting things. Mollie wondered what Angela would say if she knew that she, Mollie, had filled her stocking and not Santa Claus. It wouldn't be any use telling her, for she wouldn't believe it!

Then Santa Claus told the Wishing-Chair to fly back to

the playroom, and very soon it was there, standing on the floor.

'Goodbye, dear old Santa!' said Mollie, and she gave the jolly old man a hug. So did Peter. Binky shook hands with him very solemnly. Then they watched him fly off in their chair to fill hundreds more stockings. He waved to them as he went out of sight.

'Oh, I'm *so* sleepy!' said Mollie. 'Goodnight, Binky dear – see you tomorrow!'

They ran up the garden, crept into the house, and were soon fast asleep. And in the morning, what a wonderful surprise!

Santa Claus had come back at the end of his journey, and his last visit had been to Mollie and Peter. He must have climbed down their chimney whilst they slept, and he had filled their stockings from top to toe! They were almost bursting with good things!

The presents had even overflowed on to the floor!

'Oh, here's just what I wanted!' cried Mollie, picking up a book. '*Mr Galliano's Circus*! And here's a doll that opens and shuts its eyes – and a toy typewriter – and a doll's bathroom – and, oh look, Peter, you've got six different kinds of aeroplanes!'

Peter had plenty of other things besides those. The two children were very happy indeed. Mother was most astonished when she saw all their toys.

'Why, anyone would think you were great friends of Santa Claus, by the way he has spoilt you with so many presents!' she said.

'We *are* friends of his!' said Mollie happily.

After breakfast they went down to the playroom to wish Binky a merry Christmas – and do you know, he had as many things as they had too! So you can guess what a fine Christmas morning they had, playing with everything.

'Good old Santa Claus, and good old Wishing-Chair!' said Peter, patting the chair, which was safely back in its place. 'I do hope Santa Claus is having as good a Christmas as we are!'

Well, I expect he was, don't you?

## CHAPTER 6

## THE WITCH'S CAT

One afternoon towards the end of the Christmas holidays, Mollie and Peter were talking to Binky the pixie in their playroom. Mollie was sitting in the magic chair, knitting as she talked. She was making a warm scarf for Binky, who often used to go out at night and talk to the fairies in the garden. It was still very cold, and Mollie was afraid he would get a chill.

Peter and Binky were not looking at Mollie at all – and then a dreadful thing happened! The chair grew its red wings all of a sudden, spread them out, and flew straight out of the open door! Yes – with Mollie in it, all alone! Peter and Binky gave a shout of dismay, and rushed after it. They were too late – the chair rose over the trees, and the last they saw of Mollie was her pale anxious face looking over the arm at them.

'I say! The chair oughtn't to do that!' said Peter. 'Now what are we to do?'

'We can't do anything,' said Binky. 'We must just hope that the chair comes back safely, that's all.'

Mollie had the surprise of her life when the chair rose up

so suddenly. She wondered where in the world it would take her to. It flew a long way, and when it came down Mollie saw that a very thick dark wood lay beneath her.

The chair squeezed its way through the trees, and Mollie crouched down in the chair, for the branches scratched against her face. At last she was on firm ground again, and she jumped off the chair to see where she was. She saw, not far off, a beautiful little cottage and, to her surprise, there were pink and red roses out all round it – which was very astonishing, for it was not yet spring.

'Perhaps a fairy lives there,' thought Mollie, and she went up to the cottage. The door was shut, but there was a light in the window. Mollie thought she had better peep into the cottage and just see who lived there before she knocked at the door. So she did – and inside she saw an old witch, standing before a curious fire whose flames were bright purple, stirring something in a big green pot.

'Ooh!' thought Mollie. 'It's a witch. I don't think I'll go in.'

Suddenly the witch looked up – and she saw Mollie peeping in. In a trice, she threw down the ladle she was using and ran to the door.

'What are you spying on me for?' she shouted, in such a rage that her face went red as a sunset. 'Come here! Let me see who you are! If you are a spy, I'll soon deal with you!'

'But I'm not!' said poor Mollie. She thought she had better run away, so she turned – but the witch caught hold of the sleeve of her frock.

'You go indoors,' she said, and pushed Mollie into the cottage. She slammed the door and went back to her green pot, which was now singing a curious tune to itself, and puffing out pale yellow steam.

'Go and help the cat to make my bed,' ordered the witch. 'I won't have you peeping round whilst I make this spell!'

Mollie looked round for the cat. There was one in the corner, busily washing up some dishes in the sink. It was a black cat, but its eyes were as blue as forget-me-nots. How strange!

The cat put down the tea-cloth and ran into the next room. There was a bed there, and the two set to work to make it. As they were in the middle of it, the witch called sharply to the cat.

'Puss! Come here a minute! I need your help.'

The cat at once ran to her – and Mollie took the chance to look round. She saw that the bedroom window was open. Good! It wouldn't take her long to slip out of it and run back to her chair!

She climbed out – but in doing so she knocked over a big vase on the window-sill. Crash! The witch at once guessed what was happening. She rushed into the bedroom, and tried to get hold of Mollie's leg – but she was too late! Mollie was running between the trees!

'Cat! Chase her! Scratch her! Bring her back at once!' yelled the witch.

The blue-eyed cat at once leapt out of the window and rushed after Mollie. How they ran! Mollie reached the Wishing-Chair, jumped into it, and cried, 'Home, quickly!'

It rose up – but the cat gave an enormous leap and jumped on to one arm of the chair. Mollie tried to push it off, but it dug its claws into the arm, and wouldn't leave go.

'You horrid creature!' said the little girl, almost in tears. 'Get off my chair!'

But the cat wouldn't move. The chair rose higher and higher. Mollie wondered what she should do if the cat flew at her – but it didn't. It crawled down into the chair, hid behind a cushion there, and seemed to go to sleep!

After a while Mollie saw that she was near her own garden. She was glad.

The chair went down to the playroom, and Peter and Binky rushed out excitedly. Peter hugged Mollie, and so did Binky. They had been so worried about her.

Mollie told them her adventure. 'And the funny thing is,' she said, 'the witch's cat is still in the chair! He didn't scratch me – he hid behind the cushion!'

Binky ran to the chair and lifted up the cushion – yes, there was the cat! It opened its great blue eyes and looked at Binky.

The pixie stared hard at it. Then he ran his hands over the cat's sleek back, and shouted in surprise.

'Come here, children, and feel! This isn't a proper witch's cat! Can you feel these bumps on its back?'

Sure enough, Peter and Mollie could quite well feel two little bumps there.

'This cat was a fairy once,' said Binky, in excitement. 'You can always tell by feeling along the back. If there are two bumps there, you know that that was where the wings of the fairy grew, once upon a time. I say! I wonder who this fairy was!'

'Can't we change the cat back into its right shape?' asked Peter in great excitement.

'I'll try!' said clever Binky. He drew a chalk circle on the floor, and then put a chalk square outside that. He stood between the circle and the square, and put the cat in the middle. Then he told the children to pour water on the cat whilst he recited some magic words.

Peter got a jug of water and Mollie got a vase. Both children poured water on the silent cat, whilst Binky chanted a string of strange words.

And then a most peculiar thing happened! The cat grew larger – and larger. The bumps on its back broke out into a pair of bright blue wings. The cat stood upright on its hind legs – and suddenly the whole of the black fur peeled away and fell off – and inside was the most beautiful fairy that the children had ever imagined!

He had the brightest blue eyes, and shining golden hair, and he smiled in delight at Binky.

'Thank you!' he said. 'I am Prince Merry, brother to the Princess Sylfai. The witch caught me and changed me into a cat at the same time as she caught my lovely sister. She sold her to the Green Enchanter, and she is still a prisoner.'

'Oh, your highness!' cried Binky, bowing low before the beautiful prince. 'It is such an honour to have returned you to your right shape. What a good thing Mollie flew to the witch's house!'

'It certainly was!' said Prince Merry. 'I suddenly saw she had a Wishing-Chair out in the wood, though, of course, the witch didn't know that! I was determined to come with her in the magic chair – but I only just managed it! It is the first time I have had a chance to escape from the witch!'

'I wish we could rescue your sister, the princess!' cried Peter.

'That *would* be splendid!' said the prince. 'If we only could! But before we can get to the hill on which the Green Enchanter lives, we have to get a map to find it – and there is only one map in the world that shows the Enchanter's Hill.'

'Who has it?' asked Binky excitedly.

'The Dear-Me Goblin has it,' said Merry. 'He lives in the caves of the Golden Hill.'

'Then we'll go there the very next time the chair grows wings!' shouted Binky, Mollie and Peter.

## CHAPTER 7

## THE DEAR-ME GOBLIN

Prince Merry lived with Binky in the playroom, waiting for the chair to grow its wings again. Binky made himself Merry's servant, and did everything for him gladly and proudly. Peter and Mollie thought they were very lucky children – to have a Wishing-Chair of their own, a pixie for a friend, and a fairy prince living in their playroom. Nobody would believe it if they told the story of their adventures.

It was three whole days before the chair grew its red wings. It was one evening after tea, when Peter, Mollie, Binky and the prince were sitting round the playroom fire, having a game of snap. All four had cards in front of them, when suddenly a draught blew the whole lot together!

'I say! Is the window open?' cried Peter, jumping up. But it wasn't. He couldn't think where the draught came from when he suddenly saw that it was the chair, flapping its red wings again! Of course! They made the wind that blew the cards together!

'Look!' cried Peter excitedly. 'The chair's ready again! Come on! Is there room for us all?'

'No,' said Binky, 'but the prince has wings. So he can fly beside us. Come on – get in! I say, though – hadn't we better take a rug? It's an awfully cold night.'

The children pulled a rug from the sofa, and then they and the pixie climbed in the chair, wrapping the rug closely round them. The prince opened the door, and the chair flew out at once. Merry followed it, and held on to one of the arms as he flew, so that he should not miss the way.

'I told the chair to go to the Dear-Me Goblin's cave,' said Binky. 'I hope it knows the way.'

It did! It flew to a hill that looked dark and lonely in the starlit night; but as soon as the chair had flown inside a big cave, and come to earth there, the children exclaimed in delight. The inside of the cave shone with a golden light, though there was no lamp of any sort to be seen.

'That's why it's called the Golden Hill,' said Merry. 'The whole of the hill shines like gold inside. So plenty of goblins live here because they are mean fellows, you know, and are only too pleased to live in a hill where they do not need to buy candles by which to see!'

The children and Binky explored the golden cave. There was

a passage leading away into the heart of the hill, and the four of them walked down it, able to see everything quite clearly.

Along the passage were many doors of all colours. Each door had a little notice on it, giving the name of the goblin who lived there. The children looked at them all, but could not see the name

of Dear-Me. At last they came to the end door, and that had no name on it at all.

'*This* must be Dear-Me's cave,' said Merry. 'It's the only one left!'

So they knocked, and the door opened. A strange-looking goblin poked out his head. He wore a waste-paper basket for a hat, and had a pencil in his mouth at which he kept puffing as if it were a pipe!

'Hallo!' he said.

'Hallo!' said Binky. 'What is your name?'

'It's on the door,' said the goblin. 'I've forgotten what it is.'

'But it isn't on the door,' said Peter. 'There is no name there at all.'

'Oh,' said the goblin. 'Well, come in, whilst I think of it.'

They all went in. There was a large and cosy room made out of the cave behind the door. A fire glowed in one corner, and a small bed stuck out of the other. There was a table in the middle, and two or three stools stood here and there. There was no lamp, for the curious golden light shone here too.

'Is your name Dear-Me?' asked Binky.

'Of course it is,' said the goblin. 'Everyone knows that!'

'Well, *you* didn't seem to know it,' said Merry.

'Only because it wasn't on the door,' said the goblin. 'What have you all come for?'

'Well, we wanted to know if you have the map that shows the hill on which the Green Enchanter lives,' said Binky.

'Yes, I have,' said Dear-Me. 'But, dear me! I could not tell you where it is at the moment!'

'Did you put it in a safe place?' asked the prince.

'Of course!' said the goblin. 'But it is always so difficult to remember safe places, isn't it?'

'Well, tell us one of your safe places, and we'll look there,' said Mollie.

'It might be in that drawer,' said the goblin, pointing to a drawer in the kitchen table. Mollie opened it, and then stared in the greatest surprise. It was full of peapods, turned brown and dry!

'Dear me!' said the goblin. 'So that's where those peapods went to last summer. Well, look in the teapot, then, and see if the map's there.'

'In the *teapot*!' said Peter, thinking the goblin must be quite mad. However, he looked in the teapot on the dresser, and found it full of safety pins. The goblin was so pleased to see them.

'I couldn't think *where* I'd put those pins!' he said. 'You know, buttons are always coming off my clothes and I have to pin them up such a lot. So I bought a whole crowd of safety-pins and though I'd better keep them somewhere safe in case I lost them. So I put them in the teapot – and then I couldn't remember where they were.'

'Tell us another of your hiding-places,' begged Binky patiently.

'You might look in the boot-box,' said the goblin.

They all looked for it.

'Where *is* the boot-box?' asked Peter at last. 'Have you put that in a safe place too?'

'Oh, no,' said the goblin. 'Now let me think. Yes! I remember now – when the laundry came, the carrier wanted the basket back, so I put the clean clothes into the boot-box.'

'You do think of some surprising ideas!' said Merry. 'I don't suppose the washing will be clean any longer. I suppose this is it, under the mangle.'

He pulled out a dirty old box in which clean shirts and collars were stuffed – but except for some old potatoes at the bottom, there was nothing else in the box at all.

'I suppose you use the boot-box for your vegetables as well,' said Binky, shaking the potatoes about.

'Oh, are there some potatoes there?' cried the goblin, pleased. 'I'll cook them for my dinner then. I was just going out to buy some, but I couldn't find my hat.'

Binky, Merry and the children stared at the wastepaper basket on the goblin's head. 'Well,' said Binky, 'you've got *something* on your head – we thought it was meant for a hat.'

The goblin took the basket off and looked at it in surprise.

'It's my waste-paper basket!' he said. 'Now how did that get there? I spent all the morning looking for it.'

'Is *this* your hat?' asked Binky, picking up something stuffed full with old newspapers.

'Dear me, yes!' said the goblin, pleased. 'I must have mistaken it for the basket. I do get into such muddles sometimes. I have so much to do, you know.'

'What do you have to do?' asked Mollie curiously.

'Oh – there's getting up – and having meals – and dressing – and dusting – and going to bed,' said the goblin. 'That reminds me – it's time for something to eat. Will you have a bit of cherry-pie?'

He darted to a cupboard, opened it, and brought out a pie; but as he went to put it on the table he fell over the waste-paper basket, and smash! The pie fell to the floor and the red juice flowed out on to the carpet!

'Dear me!' said the goblin. 'That's the end of the pie, I'm afraid. Well, it wasn't a very good pie. Now, what shall I wipe up the mess with?'

He went to the cupboard and caught up a piece of paper that lined the shelf. He was just about to mop up the mess with it when Binky gave a cry.

'Wait!'

The pixie took the paper from him and shouted loudly, 'It's the map! Look! Fancy the goblin using it to line a shelf with! Just the sort of thing he *would* do!'

At that moment another goblin came rushing into the room, crying, 'Your chair's flapping its wings!'

'We must go!' shouted Binky. 'Or our chair will leave us behind! Goodbye, Dear-Me! Thanks for all the help you didn't give!'

Out they all ran and flung themselves into the chair. Prince Merry had the map safely in his pocket. To think how nearly they had lost it!

'Home, Chair!' cried Peter, and off it went!

## CHAPTER 8

## THE ADVENTURE OF THE GREEN ENCHANTER

Peter, Mollie, Prince Merry and Binky the pixie all looked eagerly at the dirty old map.

'See!' said Binky, pointing. 'There is the Enchanter's Hill. I will tell the Wishing-Chair how to get there as soon as it grows its wings again.'

'Then we will rescue Sylfai!' cried Merry.

'You can live here with Binky,' said Mollie, looking round the playroom. 'I will bring you an old rug, Prince. Let us know when the chair grows its wings again.'

But a dreadful thing happened when the chair next grew its pretty wings and flapped them in the playroom – for Peter was in bed with a cold! When Binky came climbing up the window to peep into the bedroom (the playroom was at the bottom of the garden, you remember), Mollie was ready to go – but Peter was much too sneezy and snuffly, and he was sure that his mother would be very angry if she came and found him gone. So it was decided that Mollie, Merry and Binky should go alone, and Merry promised to look after Mollie. They all said goodbye to

Peter and left him. He felt very sad and lonely.

The chair was anxious to fly off. Mollie sat in the seat with Binky squeezed beside her. The prince flew near them, holding on occasionally when the chair went very fast.

'To the Green Enchanter's Hill!' cried Binky to the chair. 'Go by way of the rainbow, and then over the snowy mountains of Lost Land.'

The chair flapped steadily up into the air. The sun shone out. Then there came a big cloud, and rain fell. The sun shone through the rain and made a glorious rainbow. At once the chair flew towards it, higher and higher into the air.

It came to the topmost curve of the glittering rainbow. It balanced itself there – and then, WHOOOOOOOOOSH! It slid all the way down it! What a slide that was! Mollie held her breath, and Merry's hair flew out behind him!

They slid down to the bottom of the rainbow, and then the chair flew steadily on towards some high mountains, whose snowy tops stood up through the clouds.

'There's Lost Land!' cried Binky, pointing. 'If we got lost there, there'd be no finding us again.'

'Ooh!' said Mollie, shivering. 'I hope the chair doesn't go down there.'

It didn't. It flew on and on. Presently a big mountain-top loomed up in the distance, sticking its green head up through the clouds.

'The Green Enchanter's Hill!' cried Binky, in delight. 'We haven't taken long! Now, we must be careful. We don't want the Enchanter to know we're here.'

The chair flew downwards. It came to a beautiful garden.

It settled down on the ground in a sheltered corner, where high hedges grew all round. Nobody could possibly see them there.

'Now, how can we rescue the princess?' asked Binky.

'She and I know a song that our pet canary whistles at home,' whispered the prince. 'If I whistle it, she will answer if she hears it, and then we shall know where she is.'

He pursed up his lips and began to whistle just like a singing canary. It was wonderful to hear him. When he had whistled for half a minute, he stopped and listened – and, clear as a bird, there came an answering song, just like the voice of a singing canary!

'That's Sylfai!' said Prince Merry joyfully. 'Come on – let's go towards the whistling. It's over there.'

He and the others crept round the tall hedge and looked about. Stretching in front of them was a small bluebell wood, and in the midst of it, gathering bluebells, was a dainty little princess!

'Sylfai!' cried Merry, and ran to her. She hugged him and then looked around her nervously.

'The Green Enchanter is somewhere near,' she whispered. 'He hardly ever leaves me. How are you going to rescue me, Merry?'

'We have a magic Wishing-Chair behind the hedge,' whispered back Merry. 'Come along, Sylfai. Come with me, and with Mollie and Binky. They are my good friends!'

The four hurried out of the wood to the hedge; but when they reached it, they stopped – for they could hear an angry voice shouting loudly.

'Come here, Chair, I tell you! Come here!'

65

'It is the Enchanter, who has found your chair!' whispered Sylfai frightened. 'Now what shall we do?'

Mollie and the others peeped through the hedge – and they saw a very strange sight! The Enchanter was trying to catch hold of the chair, and it wouldn't let him! Every time he came near it, the chair spread its red wings and flapped away from him. Then it settled down and waited till the angry Enchanter ran at it again. Once more it spread its wings and dodged away.

And then suddenly a most dreadful and surprising thing happened! The chair, tired of dodging the Enchanter, suddenly flew straight up into the air, made for the clouds – and disappeared!

'It's gone without us!' said Merry, in dismay. 'Whatever shall we do now?'

'Quick!' cried Sylfai, in fright. 'The Enchanter will come to look for me, and he'll find you three too. Then he'll make you all prisoners, and it will be dreadful!'

'Where can we hide?' said Mollie, looking round.

'There's an old hollow tree in the wood,' said Sylfai, and she ran with them to the middle of the wood. She showed them an enormous oak tree, and in a trice the Prince had climbed halfway up, and was pulling Mollie up. They slipped inside the big hollow, and waited for Binky to join them. He soon came.

The prince poked his head out and called to Sylfai, 'Can't you join us, Sylfai?'

'Sh!' said the princess. 'The Enchanter is coming!'

Sure enough, a loud and angry voice came sounding through the wood.

'Sylfai! Where are you, Sylfai! Come here at once!'

'I'll see you when I can!' whispered the princess. 'All right, I'm coming!' she called to the Enchanter, and the three in the tree heard the sound of her scampering off.

They looked at one another.

'Whatever are we to do?' groaned Binky. 'I don't see how in the world we are to escape now our chair is gone! We *are* in a fix!'

## CHAPTER 9

## PETER'S OWN ADVENTURE

Peter lay in bed, wishing very much that he could have gone off in the Wishing-Chair with the others. He dozed for a little while, and then woke up feeling so much better that he decided to get up. He jumped out of bed and ran to the window to see what sort of afternoon it was.

And, as he looked out of the window, he saw something that made him stare very hard indeed! He saw something strange flying high up in the sky – not a bird – not an aeroplane – not a balloon! What could it be?

It came down lower – and then Peter saw that it was the magic Wishing-Chair!

'But it's empty!' said Peter to himself, feeling very much afraid. 'Where are the others? Oh dear, I do so hope that the Green Enchanter hasn't caught them! How ever will they escape, if the Wishing-Chair has come back without them?'

He dressed quickly, watching the Wishing-Chair as it came down to earth and flew in at the open door of the playroom at the bottom of the garden.

He slipped downstairs and ran to the playroom. The chair was there, making a curious noise as if it were out of breath!

'Wait a minute, Chair, before you make your wings disappear!' cried Peter, flinging himself into the seat. 'You must fly back again to Mollie and the others! Do you hear? I don't know where they are – but you must go to them, for they will be in a great fright without you!'

The chair made a grumbling, groaning sort of noise. It was tired and didn't want to fly any more. But Peter thumped the back of it and commanded it to fly.

'Do you hear me, Chair? Fly back to Mollie!' he ordered.

The chair flapped its wings more quickly and flew out of the door with a big sigh. It flew steadily upwards, found a rainbow and slid down it, much to Peter's delight. Then it came to the Lost Land, and Peter saw the snowy tops of the mountains sticking up through the clouds, just as the others had done. The chair was very tired as it flew over these mountains and, to Peter's dismay, it began to fly downwards as if it meant to rest itself on one of the summits.

'You mustn't do that!' cried Peter. 'No one is ever found again if they go to the Lost Land.'

But the chair took no notice. It flew down to a snowy peak and settled itself there. Almost at once Peter spied some bearded gnomes coming up the mountain towards them, and he knew they were going to catch and keep him and the chair. He jumped off the chair, picked it up, and waved it in the air until it started flapping its wings again. Then the little boy jumped into it, and up they flew once more, leaving the disappointed gnomes behind them.

'This is my own adventure!' thought Peter. 'But it's lonely, having adventures all by myself.'

At last he saw the green peak of the Enchanter's high hill poking up through the clouds. Down flew the chair to the castle on the top. It came to rest in the very same place where it had rested before – in the sheltered place between high hedges. Peter jumped off and looked round. He thought it would be a good idea to tie the chair up, as Binky had once done before – then it couldn't fly away without him. So he tied a string from its leg to the hedge, then left it.

As he was creeping round the hedge he saw a little figure running nearby. It was the Princess Sylfai, though he did not know it. He gave a low whistle, meaning to ask her if she knew where his friends were. She heard him and looked round. When she saw him, she gave a scream, for she did not know who he was.

'I say! Don't be frightened! Come here!' cried Peter. But she ran away all the faster. So Peter gave chase, thinking that he really must catch her and ask her if she knew where Mollie and the others were. The little fairy raced along, panting, and disappeared into the bluebell wood.

She ran to the hollow tree where Mollie, Prince Merry, and Binky the pixie were hiding, and called for help.

'There's an enemy after me!' she panted. Prince Merry heard his sister calling for help, and he at once climbed out of the hollow tree and drew his sword. He would kill the enemy!

Sylfai ran to him, and pointed behind her. 'He is

coming!' she panted. 'Hide behind this tree, Merry, and jump out at him as he runs by!'

So Merry hid behind the tree, waiting, his sword drawn. Peter came up, panting and puffing, wondering where the little fairy had gone.

'*Now* I've got you!' shouted Prince Merry in his fiercest voice, as Peter ran by the tree behind which he was hiding. He pounced at the surprised boy with his sword ready to strike – and then stopped in amazement!

'Peter!' he cried. 'I nearly wounded you! How did you get here?'

'I came in the Wishing-Chair!' said Peter. 'I saw it come back home alone, and I was afraid something had happened to you all. So I made it come back again. I saw this little fairy and wanted to ask her where you all were, but she ran away.'

'This is my sister, Princess Sylfai,' said Merry, 'and this, Sylfai, is Peter. Hi, Mollie and Binky! Come out! Here's Peter – and he's got the Wishing-Chair!'

'What's all this NOISE!' an angry voice suddenly shouted. 'Sylfai! WHERE ARE YOU?'

'There's the Green Enchanter!' said Sylfai, in dismay. 'What shall we do?'

'Run for the chair!' cried Peter. 'Come on!'

All five of them ran out of the wood towards the hedge behind which the chair was tied – but will you believe it, when they crept round the hedge, there was the Enchanter sitting in the chair, a wicked grin on his face, waiting for them to come!

'Peter! Binky! There's only one thing to do!' whispered

Merry desperately. 'We'll run at him, tip him off the chair and, before he knows what is happening, we'll be off into the air. Mollie and Sylfai, keep by us!'

Then, with a loud whoop, Peter, Binky and the prince hurled themselves at the astonished Enchanter, tipped up the chair, and sent him sprawling on his face! The prince quickly picked up the Enchanter's cloak and wound it tightly two or three times round the angry man's head, so that he could not speak or see!

Whilst the Enchanter was trying to unwrap himself, Mollie and Sylfai squeezed into the chair. Binky sat on one arm, and Peter sat on the other. Merry cut the rope, and cried, 'Home, Chair!'

It rose up swiftly into the air, with Merry guiding it, flying beside it.

'We're safe!' cried Merry. 'Thank you, Peter, for daring to come on an adventure by yourself!'

## CHAPTER 10

## THE DISAPPEARING LAND

The very first day of the holidays Mollie and Peter rushed down to the playroom at the bottom of the garden to see if Binky was there.

'Binky's not here!' said Mollie, in disappointment.

'Nor is the chair!' said Peter.

But just at that very moment there came a whizzing noise, and in at the door flew the good old Wishing-Chair, with Binky sitting as usual on the back, grinning all over his merry pixie face.

'Binky! Oh, Binky!' yelled Mollie and Peter, in delight. Binky leapt off the chair and ran to the two children. They flung their arms round one another and hugged like bears.

'Oh, it's good to see you again, Binky,' said Molly happily.

'You don't know how I've missed you and Peter!' said Binky. 'Now we'll have some more adventures!'

'Well, first of all, tell us any news you have,' said Peter. But Binky pointed to the Wishing-Chair.

It was flapping its red wings as hard as ever it could, making quite a draught.

'The chair's glad to see you too!' said Binky, laughing. 'And it badly wants to take us somewhere. Come on – let's get in and go whilst the chair has its wings.'

Mollie and Peter sat on the seat as they always used to do, and Binky sat on the back. The chair flapped its wings, rose into the air, and flew off.

'Oh,' said Mollie. 'What fun it is to fly off in the Wishing-Chair again! I do so like it!'

The children leant over and looked at the towns and villages they were flying over. They knew exactly when they came to the borders of Fairyland, for Fairyland always had a soft blue mist hanging around it.

'Where are we going?' asked Peter.

'Don't know,' said Binky. 'This is the first time the chair has had a fly since you went back to school after the Christmas holidays. It's been a proper well-behaved, ordinary chair in my mother's house for weeks – now it's enjoying a good fly!'

The chair flew on and on. The children watched the towers of Giantland pass – the blue seas of Pixieland – the hills of the Red Goblins – and still the chair flew on.

At last it flew downwards. The children felt excited. Binky looked down to see where they were going.

'I've never been here before,' he said. 'I don't even know the name of this land.'

The chair came to rest in a little town. The children jumped off, but Binky still sat on the back of the chair, trying to think where they had come to.

A lot of little folk came running up. They had very wide-open eyes, long ears, long noses and no chin at all. Mollie wasn't sure that she liked the look of them.

'What is this land?' asked Binky.

'It's Disappearing Land,' said one of the little folk, smiling. 'You'll have to be careful you don't vanish.'

Mollie remembered the Disappearing Land. They had visited it once on the chair. It had disappeared suddenly just as they were going to land on it. Would this country disappear suddenly too? She asked Binky.

'No,' said Binky. 'But *we* may disappear if we don't look out! I think we'd better go off again. I don't want to vanish somewhere!'

The children sat down in the Wishing-Chair once more. But its wings had gone. It wouldn't fly at all.

'Oh!' said Binky. 'First disappearing trick! I suppose they've done that to keep us here. Now, hold hands, all of us – then if one of us vanishes the others can still *feel* him and take him along. We may as well have a look round whilst we are here. We'll remember where the chair is – just by that yellow lamp-post. Come on!'

They went down the little, winding street. The strange little folk hurried everywhere, nodding and smiling. There was a market nearby, and the children and Binky went to see what was being sold.

It was a strange village. Mollie was looking at a crooked little house with twisty chimneys when it quite suddenly disappeared and she was staring at nothing. It gave her such a shock.

Peter got a shock too. A dog with big pointed ears came running up to him and licked his fingers. Peter bent down to pat it – and found he was patting air! The dog had vanished under his very nose!

Even Binky got caught too – and he was used to strange things! He went to buy three rosy apples off a stall. He gave the old dame there three pennies – but just as he took the apples from her they disappeared into nothing! There was Binky, his three pennies given to the old dame, and his hands trying to take hold of three apples that had disappeared!

'I want my money back,' he said to the old woman, who was grinning widely. 'I haven't got my apples.'

'Well, I gave them to you,' said the old woman. 'They are not here! You can't have your money back.'

Binky was angry. He stalked off down the street with Peter and Mollie. He kicked crossly at the kerb. At once it disappeared!

'I say! Don't do that,' said Peter, in alarm. 'You might kick the whole street away!'

Binky was pleased to find he could kick things away. He kicked very hard indeed at a lamp-post. But that didn't disappear! It just stood there, as solid as ever – and Binky gave a loud yell and hopped about holding his poor toe.

Mollie and Peter couldn't help laughing. Peter leant against a shop window and roared at Binky – and then, very suddenly, the window behind him vanished and he fell over backwards! The whole shop had disappeared!

Peter stopped laughing and picked himself up. Then it was Binky's turn to laugh. Peter did look so very much astonished!

'This is a funny sort of town,' said Mollie, looking round her carefully, not quite certain what was going to disappear next. As she spoke, three chimneys disappeared off a cottage, and a door nearby vanished as well. It seemed as if everything that she looked at disappeared!

'I *am* hungry,' said Binky, wishing he had the three apples he had bought.

'Look! There's a shop selling buns. I wonder if *they*'ll disappear if I buy some!'

He walked into the shop. A pointed-eared girl sat knitting behind the counter. She put her knitting down as Binky went in, and immediately the needles disappeared. But she didn't seem to mind at all.

'Have you any currant buns?' asked Binky, looking round, hoping the whole shop wouldn't disappear before he had bought the buns.

'Yes, fresh made today,' said the girl, and she pointed to some fine big ones, with plenty of currants in, and looking nice and sticky on the top.

'I'll take three, please,' said Binky. He didn't give the girl the pennies until he had the bag of buns safely in his hand. Then he ran out of the shop and showed the buns to the others.

'Look at the lovely, juicy currants!' he said. 'Come on – let's sit down on this seat and eat our buns.'

They sat down on the seat – but it at once vanished under them, and the three of them rolled over on the path. How all the little folk of the village laughed and laughed!

'I do think the way things disappear here is silly!' said Binky, rubbing his head. 'Where are the buns?'

'In the bag,' said Mollie. 'Good thing they are, or they would have rolled in the road!'

But the buns had disappeared out of the bag, which was quite empty. The children stared into it in disgust. 'Oh, let's go back to the Wishing-Chair,' said Peter. 'I'm tired of this place.'

'Oooh, Peter!' said Mollie suddenly. 'Look! Your feet have disappeared!'

Peter stared down at his feet – and it was true, they had gone!

'Well, I can still walk all right,' he said. 'So they must be there although we can't see them. Thank goodness for that! Oooh, Binky! Where's your mouth?'

Binky hadn't got a mouth! It had disappeared!

A big wind suddenly swept round the corner of the street and took off Binky's cap. He ran after it, and Peter ran too – and do you know, when they turned round to go back to Mollie, *she* had disappeared as well!

'Oh! Mollie! Mollie!' cried Peter, in alarm. 'Where are you?'

But there was no answer. Peter turned to Binky. 'Binky! Did you see where Mollie went?'

But Binky had now gone too! There was nobody there at all.

Peter made his way back to where they had left the Wishing-Chair. He did hope he might meet Mollie and Binky there. He soon saw the yellow lamp-post in the distance, where the chair had been left.

'Good!' thought Peter, hurrying. 'I'll soon be back with the chair again – and I'll sit in it and wait there till the others come.'

But as he got nearer he could see a crowd round the chair. The strange little folk of the village were shouting to one another about it, and two of the pointed-eared men had hold of the chair.

'I tell you *I* shall have this chair!' yelled one man, and he pulled hard.

'And I tell you *I* want it!' shouted the other, angrily, and he pulled the other way.

'Goodness! The chair will be in bits soon,' thought Peter, and he ran at top speed to the crowd of people.

'Leave that chair alone!' he shouted. 'It's *not* yours – it belongs to *me*!'

Everyone looked round – but, of course, they couldn't see Peter, for he was quite invisible. They only heard his voice.

'Who are you?' they said.

'I'm Peter, and I want my chair,' said the little boy. He pushed his way through the crowd and took hold of the chair firmly. At once the other two who were holding it began to pull away hard. But Peter didn't let go.

'Show yourself, show yourself!' shouted the crowd.

'I don't know how to,' said Peter. 'I suddenly disappeared, and I can't even see myself. But I'm real enough, and if anyone begins to be horrid to me I've got fists that can hit hard. And you won't see them coming, either! Now, let go of my chair, please.'

'We don't believe it's yours, we don't believe it's yours!' cried everyone, siding with the two men who had got hold of the poor Wishing-Chair.

Peter didn't know what to do. He certainly couldn't get the chair away by himself. 'Oh, Wishing-Chair, we *are* in a fix!' he groaned.

Suddenly the Wishing-Chair decided to help matters itself. It grew its wings very fast. It flapped them strongly. It rose into the air – and with it it took Peter, who was holding it – and the two little men as well!

The crowd shouted in surprise to see the chair rise up. The two little men were full of fear. They hung on with all their might. Peter climbed up and sat safely in the chair. He had got away from the crowd, at any rate. He wondered what to do with the little men who were hanging on to the chair. He couldn't make them fall – they might be hurt.

The chair rose high up. Peter suddenly cried out in alarm. 'Hi, Wishing-Chair! Don't go home yet! We've left Mollie and Binky behind! Fly down again, quickly.'

The chair flew down at once. As soon as it was safely on the ground the two little men began to quarrel again about who was to have the chair. Peter got really angry. He pushed them both hard. They fell over.

'I wish you'd stop this,' said Peter. 'What's the good of quarrelling about *my* chair? *I'm* going to have it, not you. Leave go!'

But they wouldn't. Peter picked up a twig and rapped their hands sharply. They let go at once – and before they could take hold again, what do you think happened? Why, the Wishing-Chair most obligingly disappeared! Peter blinked in surprise, for he still wasn't used to seeing things disappear so suddenly.

Then he knew what to do. If he picked up the chair and ran off with it, the two little men wouldn't know where it had gone – for they could see neither Peter nor the chair now! So Peter felt for the chair and, quick as lightning, snatched it up and ran down the street! The two little men stared all round in astonishment, and then began to push each other.

'Just what they both want!' thought Peter, pleased. He

ran on and on and then stopped. He put the chair down just inside a field gate, sat down in it firmly, and tried to think what to do. How in the world could he find Mollie and Binky?

'If I go through the village again, yelling out Mollie and Binky's names, maybe they'll hear me and come to me,' thought Peter. 'They must be very worried, because they don't know where the chair is!'

Back he went to the village, carrying the chair on his shoulder. As he went he shouted loudly, 'MOLLIE! Binky! MOLLIE! Binky!'

Suddenly he heard Mollie's voice, answering. How glad Peter was! It came from the other side of the road. 'Peter! I can hear you! I'm still invisible. Where are you?'

'I'm standing by the fruit-shop here!' yelled back Peter. 'I've got the chair too!'

In half a minute he felt Mollie's hands touching him, and then she hugged him and felt for the good old Wishing-Chair too. 'Now we must get Binky,' said Peter. 'What have you been doing all this time, Mollie?'

'Oh, I've been looking for you,' said Mollie. 'I went back to the yellow lamp-post but the chair was gone.'

Just then someone they couldn't see bumped into them. He couldn't see them either, for they were still invisible. As soon as the person who bumped into them felt the chair, he gave a yell, and caught hold of it.

Peter snatched at the chair too. He pulled and Mollie helped him. They were not going to lose their precious chair! But the one who was pulling against them was very strong, and suddenly the chair was tugged right away, and they could no longer feel it. They couldn't see it either, of course – it was gone!

'Oh, it's gone, it's gone!' cried Mollie, almost in tears. 'Oh, Peter, what shall we do now?'

'Mollie! Peter! Is it you!' cried a voice gladly. 'It's me, Binky! I didn't know I was pulling against *you*! I just came along the street, bumped into the chair, felt it was ours and grabbed it. When I felt someone pulling hard against me, I jerked till I got it! Hurrah! We're all together again!'

How pleased everyone was! 'I've been looking everywhere for you,' said Binky, climbing on to the back of the chair. 'My word – fancy the chair disappearing too! This is a most uncomfortable sort of place. Come on – let's get away as soon as we can.'

They all got on to the chair. It flapped its wings and rose up suddenly into the air. 'Oooh!' said Mollie. 'That was quick – it felt like a lift going up!'

'Binky, how are we going to get ourselves right again?' asked Peter. 'We can't go home like this.'

'I can get some of that magic paint we once used at Witch Snippit's spinning house,' said Binky. 'Then we'll paint ourselves back again. That's easy. I'll send one of my friends to get the paint for us.'

The children flew on and on through the air until at last they were over their own garden once more. They flew down – and right through the open door of their playroom at the bottom of the garden. They were just going to shout and jump off – when they saw someone there!

It was their mother. She had come to look for them. The children sat perfectly still on the chair. They knew they were invisible and couldn't be seen. If Mother heard their voices, she would get such a shock, for she wouldn't be able to see them! Binky sat still too. He had always made the children promise that they would never, never say a word about him to any grown-up.

Mother looked round the playroom. 'I wonder where those children are,' she said. Then she walked out, almost, but not quite, bumping into the Wishing-Chair as she went.

'My goodness! That was a narrow escape!' said Peter, when Mother had gone. He jumped out of the chair. 'What a good thing the chair and all of us could not be seen today! Mother *would* have got a fright if she had suddenly seen a chair come flying through the doorway with us in it!'

'She certainly would,' said Binky, grinning. 'So would anyone! Now, I'll just send for that paint.'

He ran out. In a few minutes he was back and said that a friend of his had flown off to Witch Snippit's at once. 'Let's play a game of ludo whilst we're waiting,' he said. 'I haven't played since you went away to school. I've forgotten what a lovely feeling it is to throw a six!'

It was rather peculiar to play with people you could not see. It was even funnier to see counters moving by themselves, as the children pushed them round the board. They just had time to play one game, when there came a knock at the door.

'The paint!' said Binky. He opened the door. On the step stood a large tin of Witch Snippit's magic paint. 'Good!' said Binky. 'Now, what about brushes?'

'There are some in our paintboxes,' said Mollie, and she fetched them. 'They are very small – it will take us ages to paint ourselves right again!'

They began. They each had a paintbrush and they set to work. Binky painted the Wishing-Chair back first. Mollie began to paint herself back. Wherever she ran her brush full of paint a bit of her appeared! It was funny.

Mollie ran her brush over her left hand. At once it appeared. It was nice to see her fingers again!

'You haven't painted that little nail on your fingers,' said Peter. 'Look!'

'And *you*'ve painted all your face back except your left eyebrow,' laughed Mollie. 'You look funny!'

The Wishing-Chair was soon back again. Then Binky began to paint himself back. They all had to help each other when they came to bits of themselves that they couldn't reach. They had great fun.

'We're quite done except that Peter hasn't got his feet yet,' said Binky, and he stepped back to look at him – and do you know, he stepped right on to the tin of paint and upset it. It ran all over the floor and the floor disappeared! The paint always acted both ways – it made things disappear, or it made them come back if they had vanished.

'Binky!' You *are* clumsy!' cried Mollie, in horror. 'We shan't be able to do Peter's feet! Whatever will Mother say?'

Peter caught up a rag and mopped up the spilt paint as fast as he could. He squeezed it from the rag into the tin, and then looked at the little bit there anxiously.

'Do you think there's enough for my feet?' he said.

Binky, who had gone very red, nodded his head, and took up his paintbrush again. Without a word he began to paint in Peter's feet, being very careful not to waste a drop of precious paint. Mollie was very glad to see that there was enough.

'What about that hole in the floor?' said Peter. 'Is there enough paint left to paint it back again?'

'Just!' said Binky – and there was! My goodness, there wasn't a single drop over!

'Well,' said Mollie, as she heard a bell ring to call them indoors, 'we always seem to have narrow escapes and exciting times when we begin going off in the Wishing-Chair. I *did* enjoy this adventure, now it's all over and we're safely back again, looking like ourselves!'

'Goodbye,' said Binky. 'See you tomorrow, I hope! It's been lovely to go adventuring again!'

## CHAPTER 11

# THE OLD, OLD MAN

The Wishing-Chair had not grown its wings for a long time. Binky and the children had become quite tired of waiting for another adventure. Mollie thought perhaps the magic had gone out of it, and it might be just an ordinary chair now. It was most disappointing.

It was a lovely fine day, and Peter wanted to go for a walk. 'Come with us, Binky,' he said. 'It's no use staying in the playroom with the chair. It won't grow its wings today!'

So Binky the pixie squashed his pointed ears under one of Peter's old caps, put on an old overcoat of Peter's, and set out with the children. Jane the housemaid saw them going, and she called after them.

'If you're going out, I shall give the playroom a good clean out. It hasn't been done for a long time.'

'All right!' called back Mollie. 'We won't be home till dinner-time.'

They had a lovely walk, and ran back to the playroom about dinner-time. It did look clean. Jane was just finishing the dusting. Binky waited outside, for he did not want to be seen. But suddenly Peter turned pale, and said, 'Oh, where's the chair? Mollie, where's the chair?'

'Oh, do you mean that old chair?' said Jane, gathering up her brushes. 'An old, old man came for it. He said it had to be mended, or something. He took it away.'

She went up to the house, leaving the two children staring at each other in dismay. Binky ran in, and how he stared when he heard the news!

'I know who the old man must have been!' he cried. 'It's only Bone-Lazy, who lives at the foot of Breezy Hill. He hates walking, so I expect he thought he'd get hold of our Wishing-Chair if he could. Then he'd be able to go everywhere in it!'

'How can we get it back?' asked Mollie, almost in tears.

'I don't know,' said Binky. 'We'll have a try anyhow. Come back here after dinner, and we'll go to his cottage.'

So after their dinner the two children ran back to their playroom. They found a most astonishing sight. There was no Binky there – only an old woman, dressed in a black shawl that was drawn right over her head!

'Who are you?' asked Mollie. Then she gave a cry of surprise – for, when the old woman raised her head, Mollie saw the merry face of Binky the pixie!

'This disguise is part of my plan for getting back our magic chair,' explained Binky. 'Now I want you to go with me to Bone-Lazy's cottage, and I shall pretend to fall down and hurt myself outside. You will run up and help me to my feet – then you will help me to Bone-Lazy's cottage, knock at the door, and explain that I'm an old lady who needs a drink of water and a rest.'

'And whilst we're in the cottage we look round to see if our chair is there!' cried Peter. 'What a marvellous plan!'

They set off. Binky took them through a little wood they never seemed to have seen before, and when they came out on the other side of it, they were in country that looked quite different! The flowers were brighter, the trees were full of blossom, and brilliant birds flew here and there!

'I never knew it was so easy to get into Fairyland!' said Mollie, in surprise.

'It isn't!' said Binky, with a grin, lifting up his black shawl and peeping at the children merrily. 'You could not possibly find it unless you had me with you!'

'Is that Bone-Lazy's cottage?' asked Mollie, pointing towards a cottage at the foot of a nearby hill.

Binky nodded.

'I'll go on ahead now,' he said. 'Then you must do your part as we have planned. Good luck!'

He hobbled on in front, looking for all the world like an old woman. When he came just by the cottage, Binky suddenly gave a dreadful groan, and fell to the ground. At once the children rushed up and pulled the pretend old woman to her feet. From the corner of his eye Peter saw someone looking out of the window of the cottage at them.

'Quick! Quick!' he cried very loudly to Mollie. 'This poor woman has fainted! We must take her into this cottage and ask for a drink of water for her. She must rest!'

They half carried Binky to the cottage door and knocked loudly. An old, old man opened it. He had narrow cunning eyes and the children didn't like the look of him at all. They explained about the old woman and took her into the cottage. 'Could you get a drink of water?' said Mollie.

The old chap left the room, grumbling. 'I shall have to go to the well,' he muttered crossly.

'Good!' thought Peter. 'It will give us time for a look round.'

But, to their great disappointment, their Wishing-Chair was not to be seen! The cottage had only one room, so it did not take them long to hunt all round it. Before they had time to say anything the old, old man came back with a jug of water.

Mollie took it from him – and then she suddenly noticed a very curious thing. A great draught was coming from a big chest-of-drawers standing in a corner. She stared at it in surprise. How could it be making such a wind round her feet? It was only a chest-of-drawers!

But wait a minute! *Was* it only a chest-of-drawers? Quick as lightning Mollie upset the jug of water, and then turned to Bone-Lazy in apology. 'Oh! I'm so sorry! I've upset the water! How very careless of me! I wonder if you'd be good enough to get some more?'

The old man shouted rather rudely, snatched up the jug, and went down the garden to the well. The others stared at Mollie in surprise.

'Whatever did you do that for?' said Peter.

'There's something odd about that chest-of-drawers,' said Mollie. 'There's a strange wind coming from it. Feel, Binky! I upset the jug just to get the old man out of the way for a minute.'

'Stars and moon! He's changed our chair into a chest!' cried Binky. 'It must have grown wings, but we can't see them because of Bone-Lazy's magic! Quick, all of you! Jump into a drawer, and I'll wish us away!'

The children pulled open two of the enormous drawers and sat inside. Binky sat on top, crying 'Home, Wishing-Chair, home!'

The chest groaned, and the children heard a flapping noise. Just at that moment the old man came into the room again with a jug of water. How he stared! But, before he could do anything, the chest-of-drawers rose up in the air, knocked the water out of his hand, almost pushed him over, and squeezed itself out of the door.

'You won't steal our chair again!' shouted cheeky Binky, and he flung his black shawl neatly over Bone-Lazy's head.

The chest rose high into the air, and then a funny thing happened. It began to change back into the chair they all knew so well! Before they could think what to do, the children found themselves sitting safely on the seat, for the drawers all vanished into cushions! Binky was on the top of the back, singing for joy.

'That *was* a marvellous plan of yours!' said Peter.

'Well, Mollie was the sharpest!' laughed Binky. 'It was she who noticed the draught from the chest. Good old Mollie!'

## CHAPTER 12

## TOPSY-TURVY LAND

Once the Wishing-Chair played a very silly trick on Mollie. The children were cross about it for a long time, and so was Binky the pixie.

The chair had grown its wings and the children sat on the seat as usual with Binky on the back.

'Where shall we go?' asked Peter.

'Let's go to Topsy-Turvy Land,' said Binky with a laugh. 'It's a funny place to see – everything wrong, you know! It will give us a good laugh!'

'Yes, let's go there!' said Peter, pleased. 'It would be fun.'

'To Topsy-Turvy Land, Chair!' commanded Binky. The chair rose up in the air and flew off at once. It flapped its wings fast, and very soon the children had flown right over the spires of Fairyland and were gazing down on a strange-looking land.

The chair flew downwards. It came to rest in a village, and the children and Binky jumped off. They stared in surprise at the people there.

Nobody seemed to know how to dress properly! Coats

were on back to front, and even upside down. One little man had his trousers on his arms! He wore his legs through the sleeves of his coat. The children began to giggle, and the little man looked at them in surprise.

'Have you had bad news?' he asked.

'Of course not,' said Peter. 'We shouldn't laugh if we had!'

'You would if you lived in Topsy-Turvy Land,' grinned Binky. 'Look at this woman coming along, crying into her handkerchief. Ask her what's the matter.'

'What is the matter?' asked Mollie. The woman mopped her streaming eyes and said, 'Oh, I've just found my purse, which I lost, and I'm so glad.'

'There you are!' said Binky. 'They cry when they're glad and smile when they're sad!'

'Look at that man over there!' said Mollie suddenly. 'He's getting into his house by the window instead of through the door; and do look! His door has lace curtains hung over it. Does he think it's a window?'

'I expect so,' said Binky, with a grin. 'Do you see that little boy over there with gloves on his feet and shoes on his hands? I must say I wouldn't like to live in Topsy-Turvy Land!'

The children didn't want to live there either – but it really was fun to see all the curious things around them. They saw children trying to read a book backwards. They watched a cat crunching up a bone and a dog lapping milk, so it seemed as if even the animals were topsy-turvy too!

Suddenly a policeman came round the corner, and as soon as he saw the children and Binky with their chair, he bustled up to them in a hurry, taking out a notebook as large as an atlas as he did so.

'Where is your licence to keep a chair?' he asked sternly. He took out a rubber and prepared to write with it.

'You can't write with a rubber!' said Mollie.

'I shall write with whatever I please!' said the policeman. 'Yes, and I shall rub out with my pencil if I want to. Now, then, where's your licence?'

'You don't need to have a licence for a chair,' said Binky, impatiently. 'Don't be silly. It isn't a motor car.'

'Well, it's got wings, so it must be an aeroplane chair,' said the policeman, tapping with his rubber on his enormous notebook. 'You have to have a licence for that in this country.'

'We haven't a licence and we're not going to get one,' said Peter, and he pushed the policeman's notebook away, for it was sticking into him. The policeman was furious. He glared at Binky. He glared at Peter. He glared at Mollie – and then he glared at the chair. The chair seemed to feel uncomfortable. It hopped about on the pavement and tried to edge away from the policeman.

'I shall take your chair to prison,' said the policeman, and he made a grab at it. The chair hopped away – and then hopped back unexpectedly and trod hard on one of the policeman's feet. Then off it went again. Binky ran after it.

'Hi, come back, Chair!' he yelled. 'We can't have you going off like this. Don't be afraid. We won't let the policeman get you! Come on, Mollie and Peter – jump into the chair quickly, and we'll fly off.'

Peter ran after the chair – but the policeman caught hold of Mollie's arm. Binky and Peter jumped into the chair before they saw what was happening to Mollie – and, dear me, before they could get off it again, the chair spread its red wings and rose up into the air!

'Peter! Binky! Don't leave me here!' shouted Mollie, trying to wriggle away from the policeman.

'Chair, fly down again!' commanded Binky.

But, do you know, the Wishing-Chair was so scared of being put into prison that it wouldn't do as it was told! It flew on, straight up into the air with Peter and Binky, and left poor Mollie behind. Nothing Binky could say would make that disobedient chair go down again to fetch Mollie. It flew on and on and was soon out of sight.

Mollie was terribly upset. She began to cry, and the policeman stared at her. 'What is amusing you?' he asked. 'What are you glad about?'

'I'm *not* amused or glad!' said Mollie. 'I'm not like you silly topsy-turvy people, crying when I'm glad, and laughing when I'm sad. I don't belong to this horrid, stupid country at all!'

'Dear me, I didn't know that,' said the policeman, putting away his notebook. 'Why didn't you say so before?'

'You never asked me,' said Mollie, half angry, half frightened. 'My friend, the pixie who was here just now, will probably tell the pixie king how you kept me here, and he will be VERY ANGRY INDEED.'

'Oh, you must go home at once,' said the policeman, who was now shaking like a jelly with fright. 'You shall catch a bus home. I will pay your fare myself. I will show you where the bus is.'

He took Mollie to a stopping-place – but as the buses all went straight on, and the passengers had to jump on and off whilst it was going, Mollie thought it was silly to call it a stopping-place! It was a comical-looking bus too, for although the driver drove it by a wheel, he had a whip by his side and cracked it loudly whenever the bus seemed to slow down, just as if it were a horse!

The policeman put Mollie on the bus as it came past the stopping-place and threw some money at the conductor. He picked it up and threw it back. Mollie thought that the topsy-turvy people were the maddest she had ever seen.

She sat down on a seat. 'Standing room only in this bus,' said the conductor. 'Give me your ticket, please.'

'Well, you've got to give *me* one,' said Mollie. 'And what do you mean by saying "standing room only"? There are heaps of seats.'

She sat down and the conductor glared at her. 'The seats will be worn out if people keep sitting on them,' he said. 'And where's your ticket, please?'

'I'll show it to you when you give me one,' said Mollie, impatiently. 'Give me a ticket for home. I live in Hilltown.'

'Then you're going the wrong way,' said the conductor.

'But as a matter of fact no bus goes to Hilltown. So you can stay on my bus if you like. One is as good as another.'

Mollie jumped up in a rage. She leapt out of the bus and began to walk back to where she had started from. What a silly place Topsy-Turvy Land was. She would never get home from here!

Just as she got back to the street from which the bus had started, Mollie saw Binky! *How* pleased she was. She shouted to him and waved. 'Binky! Binky! Here I am!'

Binky saw her and grinned. He came over to her and gave her a hug.

'Sorry to have left you like that, Mollie,' he said. 'The Wishing-Chair did behave badly. I've left it at home in the corner! It is very much ashamed of itself.'

'Well, if you left the chair at home how did you come here?' asked Mollie in astonishment.

'I borrowed a couple of Farmer Straw's geese,' grinned Binky. 'Look! There they are, over there. There's one for you to fly back on and one for me. Come on, or Farmer Straw will miss his fat old geese.'

'Binky, quick! There's that policeman again!' cried Mollie suddenly. 'Oh – and he's going to the geese – and getting his big notebook out – I'm sure he's going to ask them for a licence or something! Let's get them, quick!'

Binky and Mollie raced to where the two geese were staring in great astonishment at the policeman, who was looking all around them, trying, it seemed, to find their number-plates! Mollie jumped on the back of one and Binky on to the other.

'Hi!' cried the policeman. 'Have these geese got numbers and lamps?'

'I'll go and ask the farmer they belong to!' laughed Binky. The geese rose up into the air and the wind they made with their big wings blew off the policeman's helmet.

'I'll take your names, I'll take your names!' he yelled in a temper.

He scribbled furiously in his notebook – and Mollie laughed so much that she nearly fell off her goose.

'He doesn't know our names – and he's trying to write with his rubber!' she giggled. 'Oh dear! What a topsy-turvy creature!'

Peter was delighted to see Binky and Mollie again. The two geese took them to the playroom door, cackled goodbye to Binky, and flew off down to the farm.

The Wishing-Chair stood in the corner. Its wings had

disappeared. It looked very forlorn indeed. It knew it was in disgrace.

Binky turned it round the right way again. 'We'll forgive you if you'll behave yourself next time!' he said.

The chair creaked loudly. 'It's sorry now!' grinned Binky. 'Come on – what about a game of ludo before you have to go in?'

## CHAPTER 13

## THE CHAIR RUNS AWAY AGAIN

One afternoon Mollie, Peter, and Binky were in the playroom together, playing at kings and queens. They each took it in turn to be a king or a queen, and they wore the red rug for a cloak, and a cardboard crown covered with gold paper. The Wishing-Chair was the throne.

It was Peter's turn to be king. He put on the crown and wound the red rug round his shoulders for a cloak. He did feel grand. He sat down in the Wishing-Chair and arranged the cloak round him, so that it fell all round the chair and on to the floor too, just like a real king's cloak.

Then Mollie and Binky had to curtsy and bow to him, and ask for his commands. He could tell them to do anything he liked.

'Your majesty, what would you have me do today?' asked Mollie, curtsying low.

'I would have you go and pick me six dandelions, six daisies and six buttercups,' said Peter, grandly, waving his hand. Mollie curtseyed again and walked out backwards, nearly falling over a stool as she did so.

Then Binky asked Peter what *he* was to do for him. 'Your

majesty, what would you have me do?' he said, bowing low.

'I would have you go to the cupboard and get me a green sweet out of the bottle there,' said Peter commandingly. Binky went to the cupboard. He couldn't see the bottle at first. He moved the tins about and hunted for it. He didn't see what was happening behind him!

Peter didn't see either. But what was happening was that the Wishing-Chair was growing its wings – under the red rug that was all round its legs! Peter sat in the chair, waiting impatiently for his commands to be obeyed – and the chair flapped its red wings under the rug and wondered why it could not flap them as easily as usual!

Mollie was in the garden gathering the flowers that Peter had ordered. Binky was still hunting for the bottle of sweets. The Wishing-Chair flapped its wings harder than ever – it suddenly rose into the air, and flew swiftly out of the door before Peter could jump out, and before Binky could catch hold of it. It was gone!

'Hi, Mollie, Mollie!' yelled Binky in alarm. 'The Wishing-Chair's gone – and Peter's gone with it!'

Mollie came tearing into the playroom. 'I saw it!' she panted. 'Oh, why didn't Peter or you see that its wings had grown? Now, it's gone off with Peter, and we don't know where!'

'We didn't see its wings growing because the red rug hid its legs!' said Binky. 'It must have grown them under the rug and flown off before any of us guessed!'

'Well, what shall we do?' asked Mollie. 'What will happen to Peter?'

'It depends where he's gone,' said Binky. 'Did you see which way the chair went?'

'Towards the west,' said Mollie. 'Peter was yelling and shouting like anything – but he couldn't stop the chair.'

'Well, we'd better go on a journey of our own,' said Binky. 'I'll catch Farmer Straw's two geese again. They won't like it much – but it can't be helped. We must go after Peter and the chair somehow!'

He ran off down to the farm. Presently Mollie heard the noise of flapping wings, and down from the sky came Binky, riding on the back of one of the geese, and leading the other by a piece of thick string. The geese hissed angrily as they came to the ground.

'They are most annoyed about it,' said Binky to Mollie. 'They only came when I promised them that I wouldn't let Farmer Straw take them to market next week.'

'Ss-ss-ss-ss!' hissed the big geese, and one tried to peck at Mollie's fat legs. Binky pushed it away.

'Behave yourself!' he said. 'If you peck Mollie I'll change your beak into a trumpet, and then you'll only be able to toot, not cackle or hiss!'

Mollie laughed. 'You do say some funny things, Binky,' she said. She got on to the goose's back. Up in the air it went, flapping its enormous white wings.

'We'll go to the cloud castle first of all,' said Binky. 'The fairies there may have seen Peter going by and can tell us where they think the chair might have been going.'

So they flew to an enormous white cloud that towered up in the sky. As they drew near it Mollie could see that it had turrets, and was really a cloud castle. She thought it

was the loveliest thing she had ever seen.

There was a great gateway in the cloud castle. The geese flew through it and landed in a misty courtyard. Mollie was just going to get off when Binky shouted to her.

'Don't get off, Mollie – you haven't got cloud-shoes on and you'd fall right through to the earth below!'

Mollie stayed on her goose. Small fairies dressed in all the colours of the rainbow came running into the courtyard, chattering in delight to see Mollie and Binky. They wore cloud-shoes, rather like big flat snowshoes, and with these they were able to step safely on the cloud that made their castle.

'Come in and have some lemonade!' cried the little folk. But Binky shook his head.

'We are looking for a boy in a flying chair,' he said. 'Have you seen him?'

'Yes!' cried the fairies, crowding round the geese, who cackled and hissed at them. 'He passed about fifteen minutes ago. The chair had red wings and was flying strongly towards the west. Hurry and you may catch it up!'

'Thank you!' cried Binky. He shook the string reins of his goose, and he and Mollie flew up into the air once more, and went steadily westwards.

'There is a gnome who lives in a tall tower some miles westwards,' said Binky. 'It is so tall that it sticks out above the clouds. We will make for there, and see if he has seen anything of Peter and the Wishing-Chair.'

The geese flew on, cackling to one another. They were still in a bad temper. Binky kept a look out for the tall tower – but Mollie saw it first. It looked very strange. It was sticking right through a big black cloud and, as it was made of bright silver, it shone brilliantly.

There was a small window at the top. It was open. The geese flew down to the window-sill and Binky stuck his head inside.

'Hi, gnome of the tower! Are you in?'

'Yes!' yelled a voice. 'If that is the baker, leave me a brown loaf, please.'

'It isn't the baker!' shouted Binky. 'Come on up here!'

'Well, if it's the butcher, leave me a pound of sausages!' yelled the voice.

'It isn't the butcher!' shouted back Binky, getting cross. 'And it isn't the milkman or the grocer or the newspaper boy or the fishmonger either!'

'And it isn't the postman!' cried Mollie. 'It's Binky and Mollie!'

The gnome was surprised. He climbed up the many steps of his tower till he came to the top. Then he put his head out of the window and gaped in amazement to see Mollie and Binky on their two geese.

'Hallo!' he said. 'Where do *you* come from?'

'Never mind that,' said Binky. 'We've come to ask you if you've seen a boy on a flying chair.'

'Yes,' said the gnome at once. 'He passed about twenty minutes ago. I thought he was a king or something because he wore a golden crown. He was going towards the land of the Scally-Wags.'

'Oh my!' said Binky in dismay. 'Are you sure?'

'Of course I am,' said the gnome, nodding his big head. 'I thought he was the baker coming at first.'

'You think everyone's the baker!' said Binky, and he jerked the reins of his goose. 'Come on, goose! To the land of the Scally-Wags.'

The geese flew off. The gnome climbed out on the window-sill and began to polish his silver tower with a big check duster.

'Does he keep that tower polished himself?' said Mollie in surprise. 'Goodness, it must keep him busy all the week!'

'It does,' said Binky, grinning. 'Because as soon as he's done it all and reached the top, the bottom is dirty again and he has to begin all over again!'

'Binky, you didn't sound very pleased when you knew that Peter and the chair had gone to the Land of the Scally-Wags,' said Mollie. 'Why weren't you?'

'Well, the Scally-Wags are horrid people,' said Binky.

'You see, to that land go all the bad folk of Fairyland, Goblin-Land, Brownie-Town, Pixie-Land, Gnome-Country, and the rest. They call themselves Scally-Wags, and they are just as horrid as they sound. If Peter goes there he will be treated like a Scally-Wag, and expected to steal and tell fibs and behave very badly. And if he doesn't, they will say he is a spy and lock him up.'

'Oh, Binky, I do think that's horrid,' said Mollie in dismay. 'Peter will hate being in a land like that.'

'Well, don't worry, I dare say we shall be able to rescue him all right,' said Binky – though really he had no idea at all how to save Peter. Binky himself had never been to the Land of Scally-Wags before!

The geese cackled and hissed. They were getting tired. Binky hoped they would be able to go on flying till they reached Scally-Wag Land. Mollie leant over and looked down.

'Look, Binky,' she said. 'Is that Scally-Wag Land? Do you see those houses down there – and that funny railway line – and that river with those ships on?'

'Yes,' said Binky, 'that must be Scally-Wag Land. Down, geese, and land there!'

The geese flew downwards. They landed by the river, and as soon as Binky and Mollie had jumped off, the two geese paddled into the water and began to swim. Binky tied their strings to a post, for he was afraid they might fly off.

A Scally-Wag ran up to him.

'Where do you come from?' he asked. 'Are you messengers from anywhere?'

'No,' said Binky. 'We've come to look for someone who came to this land by mistake. We want to take him back.'

'No one leaves this land once they are here,' said the Scally-Wag. 'I believe you are spies!'

'Indeed we are not!' said Mollie. The Scally-Wag drew a whistle from his belt and blew on it loudly. Binky looked alarmed. He caught hold of Mollie's hand.

'Run!' he said. 'If they think we are spies they will lock us up.'

Off went the two, running at top speed, with the angry Scally-Wag after them. They didn't know where they were going! They only knew that they must run and run and run!

## CHAPTER 14

## THE LAND OF SCALLY-WAGS

Mollie and Binky ran down the river-path, the Scally-Wag shouting after them.

'Spies!' he called. 'Stop them! Spies!'

Binky dragged Mollie on and on. They were both good runners. Another Scally-Wag, hearing the first one shouting, tried to stop Binky – but the pixie gave him a fierce push and he toppled into the river, splash! How he spluttered and shouted! That gave Binky an idea.

He squeezed through a hedge and pulled Mollie after him. Then he lay in wait for the shouting Scally-Wag. As soon as he was through the hedge Binky gave him a push too – and into the river he went, head first, for he seemed all arms and legs. The water wasn't deep, so he couldn't drown – but dear me, how he yelled!

'Come on, Mollie,' said Binky. 'We seem to be behaving just as badly as Scally-Wags, pushing people into the river like this!'

They ran on. They seemed to run for miles. They asked every Scally-Wag they met if he had seen a little boy in that land, but nobody had. They all shook their heads and said the same thing.

'There is no little boy in this land.'

'Well, it's really very peculiar,' said Binky to Mollie. 'He must be *some*where here!'

'I say, Binky, I'm getting hungry,' said Mollie. 'Aren't you?'

'Yes, very,' said Binky. 'Let's knock at this cottage door and see if they will give us something to eat.'

So he knocked – rat-a-tat-tat. The door opened and a sharp-eyed little goblin looked out.

'What do you want?' he asked.

'We are hungry,' said Mollie. 'Could you give us anything to eat?'

'Look!' said the goblin, pointing down the lane to where a baker's cart was standing, full of loaves. 'Go and take one of the baker's loaves. He's gossiping somewhere. He won't miss one!'

'But we can't do that!' said Mollie in horror. 'That's stealing!'

'Don't be silly,' said the goblin, looking at her out of his small, sharp eyes. 'You don't mind stealing, do you? I've never met a Scally-Wag who minded stealing yet! *I'll* steal a loaf for you if you are afraid of being caught!'

He set off towards the cart, keeping close by the hedge so that he wouldn't be seen. Mollie and Binky stared at one another in dismay.

'Binky, what horrible people live in this land,' said Mollie. 'Stop him! We can't let him steal like that. I would never eat any bread that had been stolen.'

'Let's warn the baker,' said Binky. But before they could

find him, the goblin had sneaked up to the little cart and had grabbed a new loaf. Then back he scurried to Mollie and Binky and gave them the loaf, grinning all over his face.

'I'm sorry, but we couldn't have it,' said Binky. 'Stealing is wrong.'

'Not in Scally-Wag Land,' said the goblin, his cunning eyes twinkling.

'It's wrong *any*where,' said Mollie firmly. 'Come on, Binky. We'll put this loaf back into the cart.'

They set off to the cart – but do you know, just as they were putting the loaf back, that horrid little goblin began to shout for all he was worth. 'Baker, Baker! Thieves are at your cart! Look out!'

The baker came hurrying out. He caught hold of Binky and began to shake him. 'You bad Scally-Wag!' he cried.

'I'm not a Scally-Wag! I was just putting back a loaf that the goblin stole!' cried Binky.

'You are a fibber!' said the baker, and he shook Binky again until his teeth rattled. Mollie ran to the rescue. She tried to catch hold of the baker's arm – but he pushed her and sent her flying. She caught at the little cart to try to save herself – and it went over! All the loaves rolled out into the road.

The baker gave a loud yell and ran to his cart. The watching goblin shrieked with delight. Mollie and Binky ran off as fast as they could, crying, 'We're so sorry! But it was your own fault for not believing us!'

They ran until they came to a field of buttercups. They squeezed through a gap in the hedge, and sat down to get their breath.

'I'm thirsty as well as hungry now,' said Mollie. 'Where can we get a drink? If we went and asked for a drink of water surely no Scally-Wag would want to steal that for us! Look, there's a cottage over there, Binky. Let's go and ask.'

They went to the cottage, hot and thirsty and tired. A brownie woman came to the door. She was a cross-looking creature.

'I thought you were the milkman,' she said.

'No, he's just down the road there,' said Binky, pointing. 'Please, Mam, may we have a drink of water.'

'I'll get you a drink of milk!' said the woman, and to Binky's surprise she darted down the road to the milkman's little hand-cart, and turned on the tap of the churn. The milk ran out of the tap on to the road.

'Come on!' said the woman. 'Drink this!'

'But we can't do that!' cried Mollie in surprise and disgust. 'That's stealing. Oh, do turn off the tap. The milk is all going to waste!'

The milkman could be heard coming down someone's path, whistling. The woman ran back to her house, leaving the tap turned on. The milkman heard his milk running to waste and ran to turn off the tap, shouting angrily. 'Who did this? Wait till I catch them!'

'They did it, those children did it! I saw them!' cried the brownie woman from her door. The milkman saw Binky and Mollie standing nearby and made a dart for them. But this time they got away before they were caught. They ran down the lane and darted inside a little dark shed to hide.

'It's too bad,' said Mollie. 'These Scally-Wags keep doing horrid things and blaming them on to us. I do hate them!'

'Sh!' said Binky. 'There's the milkman coming after us. Cover yourself in this old sack, Mollie, and I'll do the same.'

They lay down in a corner, covered with the sacks. The milkman looked into the shed and ran on. Mollie sat up. She looked at Binky and laughed.

'You do look dirty and hot and untidy,' she said.

'So do you,' said Binky. 'In fact, we look like proper little Scally-Wags. They all look dirty and untidy too! Now, where shall we go next! If only we could find Peter!'

They went out of the shed. The hot sun shone down on them. They felt thirstier than ever. They saw a little stream running nearby, looking cool and clear.

'What about getting a drink from that?' said Mollie.

'Well, I don't like drinking from streams,' Binky said. 'But really, I'm dreadfully thirsty! Let's try it. But don't drink too much, Mollie.'

The two of them knelt down by the stream, took water into their cupped hands and drank. Ooooh! It was so cold and delicious. Just as they finished and were feeling much better, they heard a voice behind them.

'That will be tuppence each, please. You have drunk from my stream.'

They turned and saw a wizard behind them, in a tall, pointed hat, and cloak embroidered with stars.

'We haven't any money,' said Binky.

'Then you had better come with me and work for me for one day to pay for the drinks you have had,' said the wizard. He tried to grab hold of Mollie – but quick as thought Binky lifted his fist and brought it down on the wizard's pointed hat. It was crushed right down over his long nose, and he couldn't see a thing!

Once more Mollie and Binky ran. 'Oh dear,' panted Mollie, 'we really are behaving just like Scally-Wags, Binky – but we can't seem to help it!'

'Look! There's the river again!' said Binky in delight. 'And there are our two geese. Let's get on their backs, Mollie, and go away from this land. I'm sure Peter isn't here. No one seems to have seen him. I'm tired of being here.'

'All right,' said Mollie. They ran down the river-bank and called to the geese.

'Come here! We want to fly farther on!'

And then, to their great surprise, a witch in a green shawl stood up on the bank and cried, 'Hi! Leave my geese alone!'

'They are not yours, they are ours!' yelled Binky in anger. He cut the string as the geese came swimming to the bank. The witch tried to grab the two big birds –

and in a fright they spread their big wings, flew up into the air and away! Mollie and Binky watched them in the greatest dismay. Their way of escape had gone!

Binky was furious with the witch. Before Mollie could stop him he gave her a push, and she went flying into the water. Splash!

'Binky! You mustn't keep pushing people into the water!' cried Mollie, turning to run away again – but this time it was too late. The witch shouted a few magic words as she made her way out of the river – and lo and behold, Binky and Mollie found that they could not move a step!

'So you thought you could push me into the river and run away, did you?' said the witch. 'Well, you were mistaken! I shall now take you before our king – and no doubt he will see that you are well punished. March!'

The two found that they could walk – but only where the witch commanded. Very miserably indeed they marched down a long, long road, the witch behind them, and at last came to a small palace. Up the steps they went, and the witch called to the guard there.

'Two prisoners for the king! Make way!'

The guards cried, 'Advance!' and the three of them, Mollie, Binky and the witch, walked down a great hall. Sitting on a throne at the end, raised high, was the king, wearing a golden crown and a red cloak.

And oh, whatever do you think! Mollie and Binky could hardly believe their eyes – for the king was no other than Peter – yes, Peter himself! He was still wearing his golden cardboard crown and the red rug for a cloak – and his throne was the Wishing-Chair. Its wings had disappeared. It looked just like an ordinary chair.

Peter stared at Mollie and Binky in amazement – and they stared at him. Mollie was just going to cry, 'Peter! Oh, Peter!' when Peter winked at her, and Binky gave her a nudge. She was not to give his secret away!

## CHAPTER 15

## THE PRINCE'S SPELLS

For a minute or two Peter, Mollie and Binky gazed at one another and said nothing. Then the witch spoke.

'Your Majesty, here are two prisoners for you. They pushed me into the river after they had tried to steal my geese.'

'Leave them with me,' said Peter in a solemn voice. 'I will punish them, Witch.'

The witch bowed and went out backwards. Mollie wanted to giggle but she didn't dare to. Nobody said a word until the big door closed.

Then Peter leapt down from the chair and flung his arms round Mollie and Binky. They hugged one another in delight.

'Peter, Peter! Tell us how it is you are king here!' said Mollie.

'Well, it is quite simple,' said Peter. 'The chair flew off with me as you know. It flew for some time, and then began to go downwards. It landed on the steps of this palace, which had been empty for years.'

'As soon as the Scally-Wags saw me, all dressed up in my

crown and cloak, sitting on the flying chair, they thought I must be some wonderful magic king come from a far-off land to live here. So they bowed down before me, and called me King. I didn't know what to do because the Wishing-Chair's wings disappeared, of course, so I couldn't escape. I just thought I'd better pretend to be a king and wait for you to come along – for I guessed you and Mollie would find some way of getting to me! Now, tell me *your* adventures!'

How Peter laughed when he heard what a lot of people Binky had pushed into the water! 'You really are a bit of a Scally-Wag yourself, Binky,' he said. 'That's the sort of thing the Scally-Wags love to do!'

'Peter, how can we all escape?' asked Mollie. 'If only the Wishing-Chair would grow its wings again! But it never does when we really want it to!'

'What will Mother say if we stay away too long?' said Peter, looking worried.

'Well, a day here is only an hour in your land,' said Binky. 'So don't worry. Even if we have to be here for two or three days it won't matter, because it will only be two or three hours really. Your mother won't worry if you are only away for a few hours.'

'And by that time perhaps the chair will have grown its wings again,' said Mollie, cheering up.

'Look here,' said Binky, 'I think you ought to make up some sort of punishment for us, Peter, or the witch will think there is something funny about you. Make us scrub the floor, or something. Anything will do.'

'But do give us something to eat,' said Mollie. 'We really are very hungry.'

Peter clapped his hands. The door swung open and two soldiers appeared. They saluted and clicked their heels together.

'Bring me a tray of chocolate cakes, some apples and some sardine sandwiches,' commanded Peter. 'And some lemonade too. Oh, and bring two pails of hot water and two scrubbing-brushes. I am going to make my two prisoners scrub the floor.'

The guards saluted and went out. In a few minutes two Scally-Wags, dressed in footmen's uniform, came in with the tray of food. How good it looked! Behind them followed another Scally-Wag carrying two pails of steaming hot water, two scrubbing-brushes, and some soap.

'Your Majesty, is it safe for you to be alone with two prisoners as fierce as these?' asked one of the Scally-Wags.

'Dear me, yes,' said Peter. 'I would turn them both into black beetles if they so much as frowned at me!'

The Scally-Wags bowed and went out. Mollie and Binky giggled. 'Do you like playing at being a king, Peter?' asked Mollie.

'I'm not playing at it, I *am* a king!' said Peter. 'Come and help yourselves to food, you two. I'll have some too. It looks good.'

It *was* good! But in the middle of the meal there came a loud knock at the door. Mollie and Binky flung down their sandwiches in a hurry, caught up scrubbing-brushes and went down on their hands and knees! They pretended to be hard at work scrubbing as three Scally-Wags entered with a message.

'Your Majesty!' they said, bowing low till their foreheads

bumped against the floor. 'His Highness, the Prince of Goodness Knows Where, is coming to see you tomorrow, to exchange magic spells. He will be here at eleven o'clock.'

'Oh,' said Peter. 'Thanks very much.'

The three Scally-Wags looked angrily at Mollie and Binky scrubbing the floor, and said, 'Shall we beat these prisoners for you, Your Majesty? We hear that they have pushed three people into the river, and smashed down the old wizard's hat on to his nose, and ...'

'That's enough,' said Peter in a fierce voice. 'I punish my prisoners myself. Any interference from you, and you will scrub my floor too!'

'Pardon, pardon, Your Majesty!' cried the three Scally-Wags, and they backed away so fast that they fell over one another and rolled down the steps. The two children and Binky laughed till their sides ached.

'Oh, Peter, you do make a good king!' said Mollie. 'I do wish I could be a queen!'

'I say! What about this Prince of Goodness Knows Where,' said Binky. 'If he is really coming to exchange magic spells with you, Peter, you will find things rather difficult. Because, you see, you can't do any spells at all.'

The three stared at one another. Then Peter had an idea.

'Look here, Binky, couldn't you change places with me tomorrow, and do spells instead of me?' he asked. 'I'll say that I will receive the prince alone – so that none of the Scally-Wags will know it's you and not me.'

'Good idea!' cried Binky at once. 'I don't know anything about the prince, but perhaps I can manage to satisfy him. That's just what we'll do – change places!'

That night Mollie and Binky slept in the kitchen of the palace. They were quite comfortable on a big sofa there, though the two kitchen cats would keep on lying down on top of them. They were nice, warm cats, but very fat and heavy. Peter slept on a golden bed in a big bedroom – but he said he would much rather have slept with Molly and Binky on the kitchen sofa with the cats. It was lonely in that golden bed.

Peter told the soldiers that he meant to keep the two prisoners, Mollie and Binky, as personal servants, and therefore they were to bring him in his breakfast. You may be sure that the two of them piled the trays up well with food of all kinds when they took the breakfast in! They laid it on a table, and then they all ate a good meal, though Mollie and Binky had to eat theirs standing behind Peter's chair, in case someone came in suddenly.

As the morning went on and the time came nearer for the prince to come, the three began to feel rather excited. Peter gave orders that he was to be alone with the prince.

'See that no one comes into the room whilst his highness is here,' he said to the soldiers. They saluted and went out smartly. Peter said it was fun to have two soldiers obeying him like that.

'Now here's the crown, Binky,' he said, handing him the golden cardboard crown. 'And here's the red rug for a cloak. Get on to the Wishing-Chair throne. I guess the old Wishing-Chair never thought it was going to be used as a throne!'

Binky put on the crown and sat down on the chair, pulling his cloak round him. Mollie and Peter stood behind him as if they were servants. Eleven o'clock struck.

The door was thrown open and in came a tall and grandly dressed prince. He swept off his feathered hat and bowed to Binky. Binky bowed back. The door shut.

Binky and the prince began to talk.

'I was on my way through your kingdom,' said the prince, 'and thought that I would come to exchange spells with you. I have here a spell that will change all the weeds in a garden into beautiful flowers. Would you care to exchange that for a spell of your own?'

'No, thank you,' said Binky. 'I have no weeds in my garden. It would be of no use to me.'

'Well,' said the prince, bringing out a bag embroidered with little golden suns, 'here is another spell, really most useful. Put a bit of the shell in this bag into an egg-cup and

say "Toorisimmer-loo-loo", and you will see a beautiful new-laid egg appear. You can have it for your breakfast. There is enough shell in here to make one hundred thousand eggs.'

'I can't bear eggs for breakfast,' said Binky. 'Show me something else.'

'Well, what about this,' said the prince. He showed Binky a strange little cap with three red berries on it. 'Put this cap on and you will know immediately who are your enemies and who are not, for the three red berries will wag about when enemies are before you.'

'I know who are my enemies and who are not without wearing any cap,' said Binky. 'It's no good to *me*! You have no spells at all that are of any use, Prince!'

'Well, what spells have *you*?' asked the prince rather impatiently.

Binky waved his hand in the air and a most delicious smell stole all round. It seemed like honeysuckle one minute – like roses the next – like carnations the next – then like sweet-peas – so that all the time you were sniffing and smelling in delight. The prince was most excited.

'That is a most unusual spell,' he said. 'I should like that to take home to my princess. She would be pleased.'

'Well, I will give it to you if you will give me a spell that is useful to me,' said Binky. 'Can you, for instance, make wings grow on this throne of mine?'

The prince looked at the Wishing-Chair and rubbed his hand down its legs.

'Yes,' he said at once. 'I can easily do that. If I am not mistaken that throne of yours was once a flying chair! I will work the flying spell on it!'

He took from his pocket a little blue tin. He took off the lid and dug his finger into the tin. Mollie saw that his finger was covered with green and yellow ointment. The prince smeared it down the legs of the chair. Then he stood back and chanted a curious magic song. The children and Binky watched in excitement. They saw the familiar red buds come – and break out into feathers! The chair was growing its wings! It spread them out – it flapped them and a draught came!

'Quick!' shouted Binky, jumping on to the top of the chair's back. 'Get in, Mollie and Peter. We can fly off, now!'

But the prince gave a shout and snatched Binky's cardboard crown from his head.

'You are not a real king!' he cried. 'Your crown is only cardboard! Stop! Soldiers, soldiers! Come here at once!'

The big door burst open. In came the soldiers and stared in amazement at the chair holding the two children and the pixie.

'Home, Chair, home!' yelled all three in the chair. 'Fly out of the window!'

The chair rose into the air, kicked out at the prince, and knocked him over. Peter kicked out at the soldiers and knocked their helmets off! The chair flew out of the window and up into the air. Hurrah! They were leaving the Land of the Scally-Wags – and a good thing too; for, as Peter said, they stood a good chance of becoming as bad as Scally-Wags themselves if they stayed there very much longer – pushing people into rivers, kicking them over, and banging their hats over their noses!

'But I quite enjoyed being a bit of a Scally-Wag for once,' said Binky, as the chair flew in at the playroom.

'It was a good thing for me that we had been playing at kings and queens before the chair flew to the Land of Scally-Wags,' said Peter. 'It was jolly nice everyone thinking I was a king, I can tell you!'

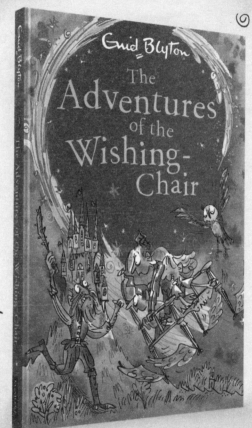

# The
# Adventures
## of the
# Wishing-Chair

**Out Now!**

**Join Mollie and Peter in the first exciting Wishing-Chair adventure from Enid Blyton!**

Available now in all good bookshops and online

# The Wishing-Chair Again

**Out Now!**

Fly away to magical lands with Peter and Mollie in the second wonderful Wishing-Chair adventure from Enid Blyton!

Available now in all good bookshops and online

# Enid Blyton

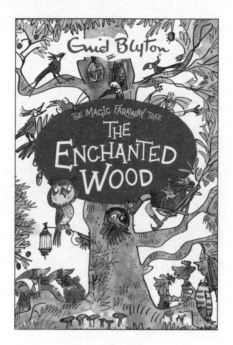

*'Up the Faraway Tree,*
*Joe, Beth and me!'*

Joe, Beth and Frannie move to the country and find
an Enchanted Wood right on their doorstep! And in
the wood stands the magic Faraway Tree where the
Saucepan Man, Moon-Face and Silky the fairy live.

Together they visit the strange lands which lie at the
top of the tree. They have the most exciting adventures
– and plenty of narrow escapes!

# Enid Blyton

*'Oh, do let's take our lunch up into the
Land of Topsy-Turvy. Oh, do, do!'*

Rick thought it would be dull in the country with Joe,
Beth and Frannie. But that was before he found the
magic Faraway Tree!

They only have to climb through the cloud at
the top of the huge, magical tree to be in the Land
of Spells, or the Land of Topsy-Turvy, or even the Land
of Do-As-You-Please!

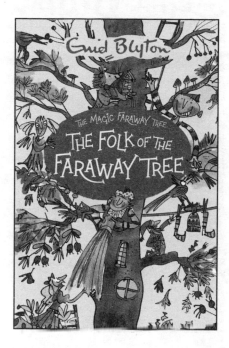

Joe, Beth and Frannie are fed up when they hear that Connie is coming to stay – she's so stuck-up and bossy. But that won't stop them from having exciting adventures with their friends Silky the fairy, Moon-Face and Saucepan Man.

Together they climb through the cloud at the top of the tree and visit all sorts of strange places, like the Land of Secrets and the Land of Treats – and Connie learns to behave herself!

# Enid Blyton

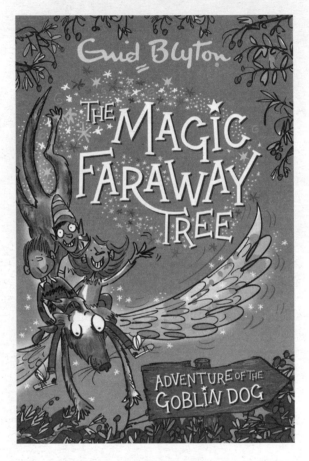

Discover the magic in this original
Magic Faraway Tree story by the world's best-loved
storyteller Enid Blyton!

# *Enid Blyton*

is one of the most popular children's authors of all time. There is an Enid Blyton book sold in the UK every minute. Her books have been translated into other languages more often than any other writer.

Enid Blyton absolutely loved writing for children. She wrote over 700 books and thousands of short stories. *The Famous Five* books, now 75 years old, are her most popular. She is also the author of other favourites including *The Secret Seven*, *The Magic Faraway Tree*, *Malory Towers* and *Noddy*.

Born in London in 1897, Enid lived much of her life in Buckinghamshire and adored dogs, gardening and the countryside. She was very knowledgeable about trees, flowers, birds and animals.

Dorset – where some of the Famous Five's adventures are set – was a favourite place of hers too.

Enid Blyton's stories are read and loved by millions of children (and grown-ups) all over the world.